# Praise for *The Many*

'Menmuir's homespun horror has flashes of Daphne du Maurier's ghost-gothic and John Wyndham's dystopia while displaying its own individuality and flair . . . Menmuir steers a steady course; the result is profound and discomfiting, and deserving of multiple readings.'
—CATHERINE TAYLOR, *The Guardian*

'The sparse prose is dark and intense, strikingly written with a haunting quality that sends shivers through the soul.'
—JACKIE LAW, *Never Imitate*

'This is a novel that has to be read at one go but one of those rare stories that once you have reached the end you start reading it all over again . . . Wyl Menmuir's style is wholly original, it grips one with its exquisitely chiselled style to create a stunningly beautiful and memorable novel.'
—JAYA BHATTACHARJI ROSE, *Confessions of an Avid Bibliophile*

'At about the two-thirds point, I started to realise that I was not reading a conventional, if slightly off-kilter and moody, story about a man having a hard time getting his life back together in a semi-hostile village. No, *The Many* is a horrific, beautifully horrific, tale that I cannot shake, as much as I may like to.'
—TREVOR BERRETT, *The Mookse and the Gripes*

'It creates an effective sense of tension and psychological suspense along the lines of Henry James' *The Turn of the Screw* but passages where the men are out fishing in the gloom also invoke feelings of intense meditation and a primal self-sufficiency similar to Hemingway's *The Old Man and the Sea*. I was slowly drawn into the novel's bizarre climate of secrecy and impending doom. *The Many* is a brisk, impactful novel which poignantly portrays grief, solitude and an inhibited state of consciousness.'
—ERIC KARL ANDERSON, *Lonesome Reader*

'The sea and the sky are so encompassing, Timothy and Ethan's emotional isolations so perfectly mirrored by their bleak surroundings, that you find yourself on tenterhooks to see what the hell is going to happen.'
—ELEANOR FRANZEN, *Elle Thinks*

WYL MENMUIR

# THE MANY

SALT

CROMER

PUBLISHED BY SALT PUBLISHING 2016

2 4 6 8 10 9 7 5 3 1

Copyright © Wyl Menmuir 2016

First published in Great Britain in 2016 by
Salt Publishing Ltd
12 Norwich Road, Cromer, Norfolk NR27 0AX United Kingdom

www.saltpublishing.com

Salt Publishing Limited Reg. No. 5293401

A CIP catalogue record for this book is available from the British Library

ISBN 978 1 78463 048 5 (Paperback edition)
ISBN 978 1 78463 065 2 (Electronic edition)

Typeset in Neacademia by Salt Publishing

Printed and bound in Great Britain by Clays Ltd, St Ives plc

Salt Publishing Limited is committed to responsible forest management.
This book is made from Forest Stewardship Council™ certified paper.

# THE MANY

# Ethan

A THIN TRAIL of smoke rises up from Perran's, where no smoke has risen for ten years now. Ethan spots it close in, a few hundred yards from shore, as he scans the houses, a regularity of grey spirals where there should be a break in the line. He turns to see if Daniel has seen it too and shouts back at his wheelman to keep his eyes on the course until they've cleared the rocks and made land.

He's as calm as he can be. He lowers his gaze and busies himself on the foredeck, kicking the empty creels and crates back into place and combing the nets laid highest for snags, waiting to feel the boat grounding through the soles of his boots.

Clem is waiting for them as they approach, knee-deep in water that could be a lake for all it is moving, holding the winch cable. He moves aside and shouts up to them a greeting or a curse that is drowned in the engine noise as Daniel brings the boat in too fast onto the beach. Ethan takes a step forward and steadies himself against the gunwale, fires a final insult at Daniel and throws a line over to Clem. By the time it has fallen into Clem's hands, the winchman has secured it to the cable in a fluid motion and is climbing up out of the water towards the machinery.

The boat's engine cuts out and the winch takes up the drone. Daniel doesn't wait for Clem to bring the ladder as the *Great Hope* pauses beyond the wave line or even for the boat to clear the water. He throws his bag onto the beach and jumps down into the water before the winch takes up the slack. He walks up over the grey stones, bag slung across his back, and Ethan decides against calling him back to finish the job. There's little enough to do and Daniel is right to want to be well away from him.

From where he stands on deck, Ethan looks past his wheelman at the smoke still rising from Perran's place. Perran, who would wait at the window for first sight of the lights of the fleet, who would run down the beach and stare as the lights attached themselves to grey shapes and the grey shapes became boats. Perran, who coupled the boats to the winch, careful and slow, and as he did this, Ethan would look over the gunwales to see the thick brown thatch of hair on the boy's head. Ethan's fingertips trace unconsciously the smooth crisscross of railroad scar lines on his right arm.

'Unnatural calm,' Clem says, as Ethan climbs down the ladder.

So Clem has not noticed the smoke at Perran's. Clem's eyes are, as they should be, fixed on the horizon from the moment he arrives at the beach in the early morning, and he won't look back towards his home until he's re-launched the boats late on. Ethan takes up a guide pole and follows the *Great Hope* up to the flat, pushing it back on course as it grates its way across the stones.

Ethan's is the first boat back and the others will limp in throughout the morning, all holds empty, he's sure of that. There's been no talk from the small fleet above the radio static. No talk until a catch is made. It's a rule. Sure as not setting sail on a Friday is a rule, sure as talking low when you spot a petrel close in is a rule, sure as not moving into Perran's is a rule.

He would like to say his father had taught him the rules, but the truth is he learned them mostly by observing them as his father and the other men in the fleet went about their business.

His memory of his father is of being told over and again the seas will be empty before he's old enough to take the helm and he remembers being told the story of a man who is cursed to fish an empty ocean for as long as he lives, the shore just in sight but never any closer. In spite of the direction he points the boat, the winds and tides conspire to push him away from the land. It's one of the few stories he can remember his father telling. Aside from this oft repeated prophesy he recalls him mostly as a silence, sitting at the window until he cast off again, or poring over the arcana of his profession, charts marked with fishing grounds long past, charts that were scored heavy with notes, advice, warnings. When he was allowed out on shorter trips on days the sea was calm, they were marked by his father's silence, by his insistence on silence.

In the wake of his father's doom-heavy story, and the absence of any elaboration, the young boy had been left to dream of a bloody exodus of the sea. In this dream fish climbed, one silver back over another, out of the foam on stunted fins, limping and bleeding over the razored rock he limped and bled over himself gathering mussels and kelp. He had dreamt of fish in numbers he had never seen and never would see, beached, panting and piled in deep drifts, staring glass-eyed over a carnage of a haul. It turned out his father was wrong. The seas were as full as ever; it was the number of edible things in it that had changed was all.

There were still fish enough to catch back then. Few and far between and hard fought over, even by the crews in the cove, but when the boats came in most times they carried catches up from their holds and there was a living to be made. There are pictures of them framed on the walls of the pub and in albums shut away in dresser drawers and in cupboards across the village. Grainy photographs of men sat on the sea wall smiling, gutting gurnard, dogfish, conger, turbot, and laying them out in neat rows in ice-filled crates. Ethan has come across them when he has searched for photographs of Perran, though he has found none, and it is hard sometimes now to bring to mind his face.

Four boats work out of the cove now. Dragged down the grey stones by Clem's rusting skeleton of a tractor, and winched back up on their return. Four where there were fourteen. And the remains of the others corrode slowly, long since stripped of tackle and anything useful and waiting to be dislodged one by one in the winter storms and reclaimed by the sea.

In the early afternoon, four men converge outside the small café on the seafront.

'You see the smoke up at Perran's this morning?' Tomas asks.

'It's emmets,' says Rab. 'Has to be. Who else'd move in there? No one who knew him.'

'Have you seen them?' asks Jory.

'Him,' says Tomas. 'Him. Just one of him. Julie saw him arrive last night, late on, in a beat-up estate car he's parked out back and then this morning he's stood in the garden, just staring out like he owns the place.'

Rab looks across from over his mug of tea.

'Been up for sale how long now?' Tomas continues. 'Looks like this time it stuck. Course it's gone to an emmet.'

'How long do you give him then?' says Rab, but no one takes up the bet and they return to their drinks and to their own thoughts.

'What's with you then?' Tomas asks Ethan. 'Sore you've lost another wheelman? Maybe teach you not to be a shit to them, you ask me.'

Ethan looks at them across the table, finishes his drink and places the mug down as careful as he can. The others around the table shrug to each other as he shoulders his coat and leaves.

Ethan starts out along the sea road towards his house, but after a few steps turns back and instead winds his way up

4

through the village to the highest row, to the houses almost at the tree line. There are lights on in many of them now, though when he gets to Perran's there's no sign of anyone there aside from the smoke that continues to rise from the chimney.

The first Ethan sees of Timothy Buchannan is a battered estate car parked on the grass behind the house, at an angle that leaves half a metre of the tailgate spilling over onto the track that runs behind the row of houses. He looks in through the windscreen, which is spattered with the evidence of a long drive. On the passenger seat is a disarray of plastic bags and part-eaten food, the crusts of a sandwich and crisps spilling out of their packets onto a map, a cardboard coffee cup dribbling dregs onto the seat upholstery. A newspaper and a blue walking jacket are strewn across the back seats and the boot is full. He can see a toolkit and some cardboard boxes with food, cloths, sprays, bottles, piled in together as though the car was packed in a hurry.

It has been a long while since Ethan has come up this way, since he has stood outside Perran's house. He walks around to the front of the house, stands at the door and listens, working out what he will say if he is confronted, but he can hear nothing from inside. The curtains are drawn, as they have been these ten years gone. Ethan walks away from the house and touches the car as he passes it, as though it might dissolve in the air like the smoke he had seen rising from the chimney.

The next day, Ethan motors out of the cove in a smaller boat he has dragged down the beach himself, and pulls up the pots on the fixed lines. It's ritual rather than function. The pots always come up empty, though the rumours and predictions the fishermen spread among themselves in the village are still strong enough to keep him coming back. He does not bother to rebait them, but rinses out the old bait and checks each of the pots for damage before he drops them back over the side.

He finds he does not want to head back into the cove and have to confront the smoke rising up from Perran's again, and instead of turning the boat back towards the village as he had planned, he steers a course along the coast for a mile or so, then heads out into open water, out towards the line of stationary container ships. The ships are spread out evenly across the horizon, as though they have lowered between them an enormous seine, an impossibly long net they are waiting to close. He cuts the engine back to a low growl and considers the line of ships for a few minutes. As he looks at them, he has the feeling of being hemmed in from all sides and a thought rises in him that he could break through the line of ships, that he could break one of the unspoken rules of the fleet. He supresses the thought, concentrating instead on the body of water in between the boat and the ships, looking for shadows in the water. He is close enough to the ships now to feel observed, though he cannot recall, even when they first arrived, ever having seen lights or any movement from the huge, rusting hulls. The men in the fleet ignore their presence as far as they can.

Ethan has been fishing for himself since he was twelve, and helming *Great Hope* since he was nineteen. With his thoughts still floating out by the container ships, looking through the wide gaps between the ships, he cuts the engine and opens the storage box at his feet. From within a tangle of netting, buoys and shackles, he pulls out a fishing rod, the one he used when his father first took him out on the boat. He threads a hook onto the line and baits the hook using some of the rotting meat he had not used to bait the pots and casts the line out. He braces the rod between the gunwale and his leg and rolls a cigarette.

'I'm fine. I'm fine.'

*Perran is still breathing out seawater from his mouth and nose*

6

*and his hair is plastered in thick clumps against his head. Though there is no light on the shore, and what light there should be from the night sky is shrouded in a thick cloak of clouds, Ethan can see Perran is shivering beneath his jumper, which is now stuck fast against his chest.*

*'I haven't found him either. We need to go back. No point now, not in this.'*

*Ethan has to shout above the wind to make himself heard. Perran shakes his head and keeps on shaking it and there might be tears in his eyes, or it might be the salt water, or the rain. The wind, howling around them, is pushing him on.*

*'He won't be out along the rocks, or on the beach. Not in this. Go back to the house. I'll go up on Lantern Street, see if he could have got up there,' Ethan says. 'Go home.'*

*Perran's gaze follows the line of Ethan's outstretched arm to where his dog may or may not be, and he turns his head back to look down the beach. It is mid-tide, though with the size of the waves and the height of them, it could be any tide. They can't see the waves as they approach, just the final white crash as the swell collides with the stones on the beach and drags them back out through the cove's entrance.*

*Perran pulls wet sleeves down over his hands and walks off in the direction of his house, though he turns back to look at the water several times. Ethan tries to conceal his concern, to reassure him.*

*'I'll find him, Perran, I will. Go on home.'*

*Ethan watches until Perran is out of sight and walks along the coast road to the turning up Lantern Street. The dog will already be back at Perran's, he already knows that. The two of them will laugh when they see each other the next day, as though their search the night before had been a joke. Ethan will ruffle Perran's hair and the fur on the back of the dog that was not lost all along.*

*He passes up by Perran's house as he makes his way home. The house is in darkness and he assumes Perran has taken himself to bed, to be up for the boats.*

In the morning, Ethan is woken by the sound of knocking at his door. After answering, and still thick with sleep, he dresses hurriedly and makes his way down to the beach, where he finds most of the boat crews standing in a huddle by the winch house. A couple of boats have launched, but the rest are uneasy going out with no Perran there and no answer at his house. No matter how bad things are with the crews or the conditions, he is always there for the boats. Always.

Later in the morning, when still he does not appear, the fishermen organise themselves into search parties, Ethan among them, and they comb the beach and the empty sheds, and then walk up through the village calling for him. Ethan tells them about the events of the night before and they reassure him that Perran will turn up.

It isn't the search party that brings news; it is one of the crews on the boats returning who calls it in. They see his yellow waders, bright against the rocks beyond the mouth of the cove, and call it through on the radio.

The operation to retrieve Perran's body is a major one. The tide is on the rise again and the rocks are already part submerged. The same rocks make it difficult to get a boat close in and the cliffs are too steep, too unstable to descend. In the end, two of the men take a small rowboat out through the cove mouth. There isn't much choice with the tide as it is, and Ethan watches with the others from the shore as the pair struggle against a sea still heavy, a hangover from the storm the night before.

When they bring Perran back in, they have covered him with a tarpaulin. The men on shore run forward and drag the boat up onto the beach and, when it comes to rest, one of the men pulls

8

*the tarpaulin back and Ethan sees he is curled up in the bottom*
*of the boat like a child sleeping.*

As the light starts to fade, Ethan reels his line back in and packs the fishing rod away. He pushes, from where they have been accumulating, a small mound of cigarette butts over the gunwale, and the congealed island of ash and paper bobs on the water and floats for a while before the waves start to break it down into its constituent parts. He looks out towards the container ships again, uncomfortable from looking down into the water for so long, and feels again the unfamiliar pull from beyond the ships and with it a dread he cannot place. He turns away from the ships and sets a course back towards the village.

Ethan is making his way in along the coast when he sees a man, his bare skin pale against the rocks on the shore a mile or so from the village, lowering himself into the dark water. He watches as the man stands thigh-deep in the sea and then he drops suddenly and his torso disappears and Ethan loses sight of him for a moment, though it is only a few seconds before he sees him climbing up the rocks towards the road.

When Ethan pulls back into the cove, Clem is on the beach and he walks down towards Ethan's boat as he grounds. They pull the boat up out of the water together, though Clem says nothing to him and he cannot find anything to say to Clem.

That night Ethan dreams of a storm in which all the boats pulled high up on the beach are dragged down the stones into a boiling sea, breaking them free of the lines that hold them to the iron rings set into the sea wall. The boats are gone faster than he can chase them and he can only watch from the coast road as they disappear, though whether it's the dark or the waves into which they break and dissolve he's not sure. He watches as the boats surface briefly in among the furious waves, and stares into the thick darkness as they are pounded against the rocks before they are dragged back. When he wakes, the stillness of the night unnerves him and he leaves the bed just so he can hear the sound of his feet on the floor.

## 2

# *Timothy*

T IMOTHY BUCHANNAN WANDERS from room
to room. In the morning light the house looks no more
promising than it had the night before, when his pocket torch
had illuminated before him peeling wallpaper and huge shadows
of stains on the walls and ceilings.

When he arrived it was late, and after wading through the
detritus in the hall, the kitchen, the living room, he had made
his way up the stairs where he found in one of the two bed-
rooms a narrow, metal-framed bed and laid down the sheet
he'd brought with him and on top of that a sleeping bag, and
slept.

Now, with more light to help him view the extent of his
foolishness, he walks again through the house, taking in the dirt
of the kitchen and the dense smell rising from the filthy carpets,
carpets that peel back where they meet the walls.

'I've not been down there myself,' the agent says. 'It's been
sitting on file for years. The gentleman who dealt with it originally has moved on from here, so there's not much I can tell
you.'

The agent sounds apologetic, but also a little bemused, as
though he cannot quite understand why someone would go to such
lengths to find a property in this particular part of the country,
so far from anywhere. Perhaps, Timothy thinks, the agent has a
slight hangover. He is young, probably in his early twenties, and

*he does not yet fit the suit and tie he is wearing. It is the suit of an older man.*

*'Do you have any photographs?' Timothy asks.*

*They are sitting in an office as grey as any Timothy has seen before, fifteen floors above street level. As he had walked into the corridor after leaving the lift, he had smelt fresh paint and the office itself carries with it a sense of impermanence, as though the walls might be taken down and reconfigured around them at any moment. As though, next week, this whole floor of the building might be replaced with a trading floor or the offices of a corporate bank. The grey walls mute what light falls in through the large plate-glass window, a window that looks out over another office block across the street, and the room is dominated by a wood-effect desk, empty and expansive. The agent is searching through a grey metal filing cabinet for information on the house.*

*'No. No photographs here,' he says. His head is almost entirely concealed inside one of the deep metal drawers. 'A few old post-cards of the cove, the village, some funny-looking rocks. You say you've been there before though?'*

*He emerges from the depths of the drawer with a thin manila file in his hand. He opens the file and, holding it at the bottom two corners, empties its contents onto the desk and picks up the sheet at the top of the pile.*

*'Deceased estate,' he says. 'Empty for ... ten years now.'*

*The agent is scanning quickly through the paper and is clearly bored.*

*'In need of renovation, it says here. I wouldn't like to say what that means really.'*

*Timothy wonders whether the agent is trying to get rid of him.*

*'No real description of the property either. Furnished, so you'll have to clear it out yourself. No structural survey available.'*

*He flicks through some of the other papers and makes a few notes in his pad before looking back up at Timothy.*

'At this price though, you can't really go wrong.'

After finding nothing that would suggest there is central heating, Timothy gathers together some of the paper he finds strewn about on the floor, compresses it into balls, and heaps the paper in the grate in the living room. He looks around for something to burn, for when he has a flame going. There are two flimsy wooden chairs beneath the window. He gives one a kick and it splinters without complaint. The thin chair legs he arranges in a pyramid over the paper. It is a mistake. The house is a mistake. In the light, the shabbiness is far from rustic or endearing, though he will tell Lauren later it is going to be perfect for them.

When the paper balls and other scraps he has assembled in the fireplace take, after several attempts to get them lit, he stands, stretches some of the remaining cold out of his muscles and pulls back a pair of stained, orange floral curtains from the window. For the first time that morning he smiles. Laid out beyond the rows of houses below him is the ocean, calm as a millpond, and a lightening sky that fades to a deep blue where it meets the horizon. As he looks out, he draws his fingers the length of the window frame and feels flecks of paint peel off beneath his fingertips. There is a thin line or crack, barely perceptible, that runs up through the window and he adds it to his mental list of things he needs to fix. He has the sudden urge to go outside and breathe in the sea and the sky.

Later in the morning, he leaves the fire burning small chunks of furniture in the grate and takes from the Volvo a canvas bag, which holds some clothes and his trainers. He changes in the kitchen and stands outside admiring the view again for a few minutes before setting off. He works his way down through a tangle of streets and runs out along the road parallel to the waterfront, his head tilted slightly to the left so he can see the water as he runs. After a couple of miles he is warm again and slows to a stop, stands and looks towards the flat horizon, his hands hanging by his side as his breathing and heart rate slow. As he looks out over the sea, he feels the need to immerse himself in the water. It is a thought he realises has been there since he arrived in the car the evening before, that he would swim in the sea. Perhaps he will start a habit he could continue long into the future, like the swimmers he has watched so often while running along the towpath beside the Thames and around the Serpentine, who day after day and year after year lower their ageing bodies into the water, drawing from it something he felt he wanted. Maybe this will become an obsession he can cultivate, a story that others will tell about him.

'Of course, you know Timothy. You'll see him diving in off the rocks out past that last house over there if you're up early enough to catch him. Seriously. Every morning, day in day out since the day he arrived. Runs at first light, strips off and swims out through the surf, rain, wind, snow, sun. Plenty of times we thought we'd find him washed up on the rocks, but he always comes back fine. He's a strong one. Knows the sea better than he knows his own wife, I reckon.'

But he is getting ahead of himself. The village is now out of sight behind him and there is no one to be seen and he takes off his trainers, socks and running shirt. He sees himself diving from the rocks straight into the water and striking out with a confident front crawl, but as he climbs down the rocks and gets closer to the edge, he sees the sea is green and shallow for several feet before it drops off into darker water.

The February water is a shock as he lowers himself into it and he wades in as far as the ledge, where the water rises up to his thighs. He stands there a moment, and looks out to sea. He could turn back now and he would have been in the water and maybe that is all he needs to do. He pushes himself off into the deeper water, breathes in sharp and hard and against his will, and feels the muscles in his chest contract as the water rises up above his stomach. He tries to turn himself back towards the shore as the freezing water comes up over his shoulders. And then he is in up to his neck and he is kicking hard back towards the ledge, pulling air back into his lungs. The rocks in the ledge cut his knees and shins as he pulls himself up into the shallows and he climbs out of the water on feet he can no longer feel and makes his way back to the small pile of clothes, clothes which are surely further away than they were when he took them off.

He dries himself as best he can with his running shirt, puts it back on and tries to stop the uncontrollable shivering that is now taking hold. As he pulls his socks on over numb feet, he sees they are cut and bleeding. He jumps on the spot a few times and wraps his arms around his chest and then sets off back towards the village.

By the time he reaches the door of the cottage he is limping on feet he feels now only as a formless ache. Inside again, he wraps himself in a blanket from the car and sits in front of the fire on a patch of threadbare carpet. As his feet warm up again, he rubs the soles of his feet on the threads of the carpet where coals had rolled off the grate at some time and burned through.

*It is a blazing hot, late October afternoon, too hot for the time of year. It's almost six months since he first met Lauren, and their first holiday, three days out of season on the coast, a precursor to him asking her to move out of her flat and into his.*

*They are too early to book into the small hotel so they park the car in the car park and head straight down to the shore. When they arrive, Lauren looks dubious. The beach has an industrial look about it. Grey stones over which lies a thin coating of diesel, dropping steep down towards the sea, which looks unnaturally calm under the same film of oil. There are a few rusting hulls* on the hard standing below the road, and bisecting the beach is a chain which runs up into the mouth of a stone building, in which he can see a heavy winch, and everything looks shut up, closed down. The beach is overlooked by a tangle of houses, packed together in tight rows above, silhouetted by the late morning sun.

Lauren gives him a look and he asks her to trust him. He knows what he's doing and he will find the right place. Before they set off that morning, he had spent an hour with an Ordnance Survey map spread out across his kitchen table scouting the beach and the perfect spot. He tells her a story about an orienteering and camping trip with school when he was twelve, though leaves out the part where he and a small group of friends became lost and, with the light fading, had flagged down a car to ask for directions. Somewhat sheepishly, they had ended up accepting a lift to the gates of their campsite from the elderly couple who had stopped for them, accepting too the handful of sweets that had been dug out for them from the glove compartment to see them through the cold night.

They make their way round to the right of the beach and Timothy helps Lauren up over the rocks, towards the mouth of the cove, and they have to jump over small inlets where water rushes beneath and into the land and Lauren looks nervous.

'Trust me,' he says and takes her hand again.

A tiny sandy beach hidden among the rocks, a speck of yellow on the map. It is there too, out of sight of the mouth of the cove, though when they arrive, the waves have already covered the sand and painted it light green. Instead, they spread a blanket on the rocks overlooking the submerged beach and look down into the green water. The picnic, he remembers too late, has not made it beyond his mental shopping list, and what food they have brought with them is still in the boot of the car. They sit on the rocks and eat the fruit gums he has in his pocket and drink what is left of

Lauren's bottle of water and she lies back against him and they talk and stare out at the white peaks on waves as far as they can see, peaks made whiter by the bright sunlight.

Timothy will not later remember the argument that ensues when they turn back towards the cove to find themselves now cut off by the rising tide, but cannot forget the hours in which they slowly back closer and closer to the cliff face as the sea rises around them.

At first they laugh. They are going to end up like one of those couples from up country who are caught out by the tide and have to be rescued by helicopter. Their rescuers will be a dedicated and earnest team who will try to hide their true feelings about the waste of time and money the couple represents. They will both be embarrassed and apologise profusely, and feel admonished and exhilarated. But when they try their phones, neither of them is able to get a signal, and they are overlooked now by no one. There is not even a boat other than a container ship way, way out, sitting static on the horizon.

The sun disappears over the top of the cliff face and what is left of the afternoon's heat soon dissipates. Timothy wraps Lauren in his coat and puts his arms around her, partly to keep her warm and partly for his own warmth. Later, he decides to attempt the cliff. It is only a few feet higher than he can reach up and he makes it halfway before a ledge beneath his feet crumbles and he slides down and he is glad he did not bring more of the cliff down with him. He puts his arms back around Lauren, and she complains to him about his getting mud on his jacket. They cling together on a flat rock a metre square and the tide peaks a few inches below their feet.

It's a hungry, frayed couple that walks back up the beach towards the hotel, several hours after the time they had arranged to check in.

Later in the day, aware what food he has brought with him, beyond the remains of the sandwiches he packed for travelling, is packed in boxes in the boot, Timothy goes out to the car and retrieves a waterproof coat from the back seat and walks down between the tight rows of houses to the shore. He pulls his collar up against the fine rain now blowing in from the sea and as he passes along the narrow streets, he feels he is observed through the curtained windows, though at a distance, as a nurse would observe a patient. As he approaches the village shop, he slows. Outside the shop is a huddle of people, two women in striped aprons and beside them two men and another woman. They are deep in conversation and when they see him their conversation ceases and five heads turn towards him. He feels foolish under their gaze and smiles apologetically, as though he has found himself in the wrong place or has taken a wrong turning. Unwilling to submit to their stares any further, he turns away from them and takes a footpath that continues down the hill between two of the houses closest to him.

When he reaches the beach, he finds the same grey stones, the same stacks of empty lobster creels and long coils of frayed rope in tall piles by the sea wall, topped with a mat of green through lack of use. The same quietness too. There is no one else on the shore, though he can see a boat in the middle distance, beyond the entrance to the cove. And as he looks back up towards the house – his house – he can see no signs of life, no walkers with dogs or runners pounding the coast road, no couples nesting down into the beach out of eyesight of their parents, no doors or windows open in the houses between here and the bare hilltop above the village.

He sits on his heels a few feet from the water, watching the almost imperceptible lapping of the sea on the stones, and feels a wave of anger cross him, anger he had hoped had been excised by the run and the shock of his immersion into the sea. He picks up a handful of the smooth grey pebbles and hurls them into the still water. He watches the ripples as they spread out, intercept each other, distort and fade back to stillness. It is a mistake.

# 3

## Ethan

THROUGH GAPS IN curtains and in stolen glances as they come within sight of Perran's, the village watches Timothy as he passes on his walks and runs, and as he carries out, over the period of several days, the tattered contents of Perran's house. They watch as he drags out a filthy carpet, which they see he has hacked at to make it small enough to roll and carry. He emerges from the house with arms full of dusty wallpaper and curtains and struggles under the weight of a rusting refrigerator as he hauls it out through the kitchen door to join the pile of furniture in front of the house. Some of the younger villagers speculate Timothy will set light to the pile like a beacon, as they do on the hilltop above the village once a year midwinter, though he never does and the teenagers don't have the bottle to do it themselves. As Ethan thinks on it, he wonders whether he might have done so at one time.

Those who remember Perran well look past or above the pile of furniture, and think they do so out of respect for him, though it is more for their sense of disgust and shame at the state of the items they see laid out in the harsh winter light, and they do not talk of it. The pile of rubble in the garden increases in size, and then, as rapidly, reduces until it is gone, and all that's left of it are small ribbons of linoleum, coloured paper and plastic, which catch in the branches of the hedge at the foot of the garden like tributes to an old god.

They see Timothy at Perran's windows as he strips back paint from the sills, as he breaks up tired furniture in the garden, and as he runs out and back along the coast road. They count the minutes or sometimes the hours he is gone and obsess over where he might be until he returns and talk about him in the café and the pub. Ethan tries to keep his eyes on the horizon, away from Perran's house, and avoids being drawn into conversation about the incomer, though he follows him more closely than any of the others. He avoids everyone during this time and sticks to his solitude and his boat, torn between staying to watch what Timothy will do next and the desire to be far away from him and from the memory of Perran.

The regulars wait for Timothy to appear in the pub and they are affronted when he stays away. They see him standing in front of Perran's house, looking out to sea, and sometimes down by the rocks on the shore's edge. He is fodder for rumour and they know so little of him, and stories emerge as to who he is, this newcomer who arrived late one night and shut himself away in Perran's house, gutting away at it as hard as the men in the photographs gut fish on the beach wall.

They lower their voices when Ethan is close by, he notices, out of respect, or awkwardness, he is not sure, but he hears the stories as they spread. Timothy has come to resurrect Perran. He has come to destroy Perran's house, to erase his memory. He's come because that's what upcountry folk do, to replace the drudgery of the city with that of the coast. He has come to save them from themselves, or to hold up a mirror to them and they will see themselves reflected back in all their faults and backwardness. He has come to change them, to impose himself on them, to lead them or to fade into their shadows.

When the boats leave in the evening, the crews see the lights on at Perran's and when they return in the morning darkness they see the lights are on still, when there are no others lit in the village, and they speculate as to who he is and what he is doing here.

Timothy's car disappears sometimes for days at a time and the village counts the hours until it returns, usually late at night, sometimes with lengths of wood strapped to the roof, with boxes in the boot, and always fuller than when it left. A few weeks after Timothy first appears in the village, the car returns with a trailer, on which arrives a table, two small wardrobes, a small bookcase and a chest of drawers.

The first time Ethan sees Timothy Buchannan up close is out past the village on a blowy mid-morning, early December. Ethan had seen Timothy leave Perran's by the side gate and now follows him at a distance further up the hill. He loses sight of Timothy and almost walks past him, but sees the bright blue of his walking coat a few minutes later. Timothy is crouching beneath one of the field walls off the track at the top of the hill, protecting himself from the rain-heavy wind. With the hood on his waterproof up, he is talking into a mobile phone, his voice raised against the wind, and Ethan hears fragments of the conversation as he walks past.

'It, it still needs work . . . Yes, a bit . . . Okay, a bit more than a bit, a lot . . . How are you feeling? And? When are you going to come? Yes, it's getting there. Yes, still some to go . . . I know, I know, you too.'

Timothy has not noticed Ethan's approach and Ethan slows his pace as he continues up the track away from the village.

'No, it won't be ready by then. I'll come back for a few days and we can spend it together. Promise. I know. I want you to be here too. Just a bit longer, I'll make it right.'

There is a silence and then 'Shit. Shit. Shit.' Timothy unfolds his limbs from their crouch by the wall and emerges from behind the stone wall, waving his phone in the air as though he will be able to catch a signal from the passing wind.

Ethan walks a way further before turning back on himself and down towards the village again and when he passes the wall again he sees Timothy has gone.

The afternoon finds Ethan on the beach looking out at the container ships three miles off shore; skeletal for their lack of cargo, idle sentries to an empty coast. The ships come in and out of view as pulses of rain and cloud push through to the shore, whipping up the spray and the waves. He cannot settle and alternates between looking out at the horizon and glancing up towards Perran's, as though a magnet drawing his gaze that way is being turned on and then off again by a bored child.

Clem, keeper of the boats and their crews, has refused to operate the tractor and they are confined to the shore, as the container ships are confined to their positions on the horizon. There are children in the grounded boats now, some in the derelicts, crawling over the rusted and storm-damaged hulls, and some in the working boats, swinging themselves up onto the roofs of the cabins and throwing loose pieces of tackle at each other across the gaps in between the boats.

They don't play in the water any more. There's no playing or swimming in the water, not if you don't want to end up sick, or sterile. A *profusion of biological agents and contaminants* is how the Department for Fisheries and Aquaculture described it in one of their many communications, a note which is now affixed with the others, mouldering on the notice board in the winch house.

After Perran died, there had been talk of Clem taking over his house, it having the clearest view of the boats returning and Clem's having none. But Clem resisted, said Perran's place needed rest after the grief the house had seen. He didn't say it would feel like bad luck to move in there and no one else pressed the case. Anyway, he had a radio and they could raise him on that of a morning if they needed to.

Later in the day the worst of it has passed, leaving behind light rain and a low tide. The waves are untidy and unsettled by the memory of the earlier storm and a group of children is gathered on the beach, armed with sticks. They are crowded round a huge jellyfish washed up onto the stones. It is spread flat, about six feet across, transparent and run through with thin red veins. The children bounce stones off its back and dare each other to touch the body, though the furthest they dare go is to poke at it with their sticks.

Clem is already pulling the first of the boats down the beach behind the tractor and the crews are in various stages of preparation, having spent much of the afternoon in the pub. Where there are jellyfish, there are fish behind. The crews take any sign they can.

Only Ethan is launching alone. After Daniel he hasn't found anyone else willing to go out and he's back to fishing alone and each launch now is marked by an argument with Clem. Whether or not Ethan can handle the two-man boat without help, whether he should go out at all, whether he is clear enough, focused enough to fish, and he tells Clem damn you to hell and operate the tractor. Clem, for his part, doesn't put up too much of a fight. He's said his piece and Ethan's not the first fisherman to ignore his advice. The other three skippers know Ethan well enough to steer well clear.

Standing up on the sea road, Timothy looks down onto the beach, his coat collar pulled up around his ears, and Ethan wonders what type of omen this is, what effect the incomer's gaze will have on the trip.

As the boats leave the mouth of the cove, they sail through a bloom of jellyfish, iridescent clouds of them gathered in the churning water. And though the boats sail out a fair way from the shore and the bloom thins, they don't clear it, and every man curses under his breath in the knowledge of what is to come.

No fish, no fish, no crabs, no shrimp nor shark, just jellies. Jellies tangled in the nets, that burn and sting and leave criss-cross patterns on arms and hands, long white welts from fronds that stick and burn and scar. It's been a rite of passage in the village since before Ethan's father was a boy.

*Ethan, Rab, Tomas and Jory are on the far rocks at low tide gathered round a thin, stringy jellyfish washed up on the rocks. Its network of nerves shows blue through the transparency of its body. Ethan wants to back down now, but they have already discussed this. It is his turn, the last of the four. Rab and Jory, as the strongest, hold him until he stops struggling. Then Tomas pulls up the sleeve of Ethan's shirt on his right arm and he and Jory hold the arm still while Rab puts a hook through the jelly and holds it up in the breeze. Jory and Tomas hold the arm tight and Rab raises the jelly up and draws its long fronds back and forth over Ethan's naked arm. The breeze is offshore so it doesn't carry the sounds of the screams back towards the houses, and instead his cries drift out over the waves and mingle with the shrieks of the sea birds.*

No fish, no fish, no shrimp nor shark, just jellies. Ethan, one hand on the wheel, the other steadying himself against the cabin wall, looks out to the spaces in between the sentinels, the unmoving container ships, tied to their positions by miles of red tape issued and reissued endlessly by a faceless, disembodied authority. It makes him think of Timothy, of his arrival into their lives, of his imposition on them. He fights the temptation to point the boat out between two of the container ships and push out through to the other side where the fishermen do not go, away from the memories Timothy has brought in with him, away from Perran.

The radio crackles into life.

'*Idler*, this is the *Idler*. We've got a catch.'

Though it is Jory talking over the radio, Ethan sees only

Timothy in the words that spring out over the static. He near as runs back to the helm and pulls the *Great Hope* round in the direction of where Rab and his crew are already lowering their nets and he makes his course windward of them, jams the wheel in position and sets about at the back of the boat to lower the net he's got in place.

He drops and pulls the net twice empty and it is only the sight of bodies being pulled up into the boats around him that keeps him shooting it again. The third time he raises the net he knows he has landed something by the change in the drag and the weight just before the bulk of the net surfaces, dark bodies thrashing about in the bottom of the gathered net amid the jellyfish. He swings the catch up over the deck with the pole, and drops it down gentle as he can and unfolds the net, avoiding the fish as they arch their backs on the deck.

He shifts the jellyfish to the side with the pole and flicks them back over the side of the boat before he inspects the catch. The dogfish look burned, as though with acid, their eye sockets elongated and deep, showing through to the bone at the edges and there are white lesions down the side of each body. Their rough black skin is dull and flaked away in patches, the fins thin and ragged where there should be muscle, and he looks each one over quickly before dropping them down into the hold. By the time he is finished, he's tired to the bone and several times he drifts too close to one of the other boats and they shout over to him to shift before he holes someone.

The radio is busy with chatter and the sound is as unfamiliar to Ethan as is the catch in the hold. Ethan does not join the others comparing catches, though he lifts the hatch several times to check the fish are still there. He rests a while and stares out again beyond the container ships while the others drop their nets over and again, though their luck is out now and none of them catches anything more before they give up and head back to shore.

There are several cars and vans parked up on the coast road when they arrive back into the cove and Clem radios in to tell them he has sold the fish before any of the boats make the shore. Ethan wonders who would buy this half-dead catch the sea has thrown up. Not restaurants, he's sure of that. Perhaps the pharmas, hoping to extract god knows what from them. Either way, he is glad he did not have to conduct the deal and, as the fish are being lowered down from the deck, he asks Clem who the buyer is. Clem nods his head up to a dark blue executive-type car parked up on the road. Two men are standing by a silver van parked beside it and stacked beneath the shuttered hatch in the side are several white industrial boxes. The two men are watched by a woman dressed in a long grey coat and they exchange words. The three of them look out of place in the village, the men in suits too light for the season and at odds with their surroundings as they ferry the crates down to the beach.

After the boats have all been pulled up above the high tide mark, Ethan sees one of the younger fishermen is sitting with a blanket wrapped around his shoulders, on the hard standing, shaking and retching onto the concrete floor in between his feet.

*They stay out on the rocks late into the night, through Ethan's long hours of vomiting and sweating and swearing at the other three boys, who alternate between laughing at his self-pity and bringing up water to cool the burning on his arms. After he has screamed long enough, and asked them and pleaded, scared about what will happen if they do nothing, he holds his arm out and the other three boys piss on the rows of white welts criss-crossing his forearms and though he swears and curses at them, he thanks them too for the relief from the pain it brings him.*

'Santo here got tremors after he caught a jelly, didn't he?' says Jory grinning when he sees Ethan looking over at the boy. 'Dropped off the net as we pulled it up and wrapped up nice round his arm like a bracelet, and he didn't like it too much. I've told him, piss on it. Told him we'll all piss on it, but he won't listen to me. Thinks I'm a sick bastard.'

'Who am I to argue with that?' Ethan says.

Jory shoots Ethan a look, grins again and returns to pulling out his remaining crates from the hold and passing them down to Clem, and Ethan looks in to see whether the other man has fared better. Jory's fish are in no better state than the ones Ethan brought back. Larger than they have seen in a fair while, but in bad shape all of them, half-dead before they were even landed. Ethan feels they have done these fish a service, by bringing them to an end, by pulling them out of the dark streams and channels into which they have strayed. Jory is happy with the catch. Says they all should be. They're to be paid for the catch sight unseen, and once they're in the van they're someone else's problem. What they do with the fish from there is their own business, that's clear enough.

Ethan busies himself unloading his boat, but looks up when he hears raised voices on the beach. Rab and one of the men in suits are stood, face to face, a little way off from the boats.

'It's all the fish,' the incomer is saying. 'Not just the ones you feel like handing over.'

'One fish,' Rab says. 'One fish is all. One fish out of how many? Two hundred? Three hundred?'

Ethan lowers his gaze to the dogfish that lies on the ground between the two men. It is barely visible against the dark beach. The man leans in close to Rab and speaks to him in a voice too low to be overheard. When he is finished, Rab looks up briefly towards the *Great Hope*, before stepping away from the fish and looking away down the beach, while the man kneels and pulls out a clear plastic bag from a pocket in his suit. He puts his hand into the plastic bag, picks the fish up, and inverts the bag, tying it at the top. He handles the fish carefully, as though it is something precious, but holds it away from his suit as he brings it back towards the boats.

'Is that all of them?' he asks Clem as he lays the fish into one of the crates. 'The agreement is for all the fish. I don't want to hear you've been holding any back. That's what the full payment's for.'

He talks quietly, and Ethan feels a threat sitting behind his words. Clem nods to the man and says yes, they have all the fish now, and in response, the man reaches into his suit jacket pocket and hands over a roll of cash

'Who are they anyway?' Ethan says, as the two men walk off up the beach towards the woman in the grey coat, who has not moved from her place by the car. 'They looks more suited to a funeral, or an office, than buying fish off the boats.'

'You want to keep your thoughts to yourself,' says Clem. 'She bought the whole catch, and you won't complain when you get your share. Or maybe it's nothing to you. Either way, I'd stay quiet about it.'

The other cars and vans have already started to move off, though a few people have stayed around to see the fish come down off the boats. The two men have the white boxes of fish in stacks beneath the now open shutters in the van and have opened each for the woman to look into. The woman in grey kneels for a while by each box before indicating the men can seal them up and load them into the van. There are many boxes in the stacks and she looks each one over carefully, as though she is looking for something in particular, and the two men look impatient.

Later, as they unload their gear from the boats, Ethan looks up again to see whether they are still there. The woman is no longer there, waiting in her car perhaps, and the two men are securing the last of the crates next to the van. He sees Timothy there too. Not standing with the men loading the van, but standing close to them, by the railings above the beach. Timothy is trying to conceal his shock at the state of the black fish. He looks transfixed by the sight of the mutated haul, and the men loading the boxes onto the van cover the remaining crates sitting on the roadside with a tarpaulin. Ethan feels a flash of compassion for Timothy and turns back quickly to folding his nets and stowing them. He sees the other crews have seen Timothy there too and they are looking up at him with new expressions.

The others finish up on their boats quickly, and head over to the pub to celebrate their catch and Ethan considers joining them, but instead finds himself walking up again towards Perran's, though when he gets there he sees no sign of Timothy, only the evidence of his continued work on the house.

Later, when he gets back to his own house, Ethan falls onto his bed and into a deep sleep. In his dream he is sailing the *Great Hope* over a glassy sea. The deck is clear of all the paraphernalia of fishing and the boat looks refurbished and renewed, newly painted and smooth. He is not at the helm and there is no sound of an engine, though the boat moves through the water and out into a wide sea. He is looking over the side of the boat into clear water when he sees the flank of a great creature pass beneath the boat, muscular and immensely long. He looks round, but there is no one else on board to tell and no method he can think of to record this happening. He returns his gaze to the water, in time to see the creature's great flukes pass by beneath, and he watches it retreat and become formless, a fading shadow merging itself with the darkness of the deeper water.

The next day, Perran's house is shut up and the battered car is gone. With Timothy absent, the house seems to look no different to the way it had before he arrived, as though it has relaxed back into its former state. Ethan watches for Timothy's return all that day and all the next and does not go back out to sea, as though Timothy has taken his desire to fish with him in the boot of his car. Sensing the change in Ethan, the other three skippers start to head to the pub instead of to their boats. They blame the shortness of the days, the shortness of the prospects, and the weather, but really they need little excuse and for two weeks most of the village forgets about Timothy Buchannan.

# 4

# *Ethan*

B Y EARLY JANUARY, the *Great Hope* has returned to the water and is the only boat sailing from the small cove. The other skippers remain at the bar and tell each other stories of catches they themselves have never made and of storms they have only watched from the shore.

Ethan spends long hours carving furrows into the dark sea, furrows that close over behind him as he passes. Each time he leaves the beach, he does so with a sense of determination that quickly weakens. Some days he drops his nets, but mostly he just motors out and cuts the engine, glad to be away from the village and from the talk. With nothing else to occupy him, his thoughts return over and again to the memories Timothy's arrival have drawn up. When he is forced to return to the village, when the cold has crept down inside his jacket and fixed itself there, or when the light on the fuel gauge calls out to him, he heads back in and avoids looking at the rocks on either side of the entrance to the cove, for fear of seeing, as he has seen so many times in his head, the flash of bright yellow that had led the fishermen to Perran. It seems to him that Timothy's arrival has brought Perran's death back to the village somehow, though he is unsure how this could be.

He keeps watch on the chimney at Perran's and on the coast road, for the sight of the newcomer's battered car, hoping his return will bring with it fish, even if they are pulled up mauled and half-dead. He imagines the fish will sense Timothy's return as he drives back towards the village. He sees them dragged up in great numbers from whatever depths at which they hide, in currents below the reach of the chemicals, and that Timothy will drag with him, as though with an invisible net, a broad lane, tight with shifting, seething bodies, that twists unseen alongside him as he comes back into the village.

But as he looks out over the expanse of sea towards the coast, he sees no sign of Timothy's return, and no sign of the shadow the fish cast on the surface of the water, no sign of their struggle as they fight against the currents.

He realises then he is not fishing but hunting, and he watches for Timothy the way a hunter waits for a stalked deer. He watches the bare landscape for Timothy's return and forgets the purpose with which he came out on the water.

On a day the sun does not manage to rise fully above the horizon, shining a weak light between the land and dark clouds overhead, he sits on the deck on a crate and feels the swell of the ocean beneath the boat. He is watching a figure move across the land. It is a while before he realises it is Timothy running out along the coast road, a pale figure against the dark fields.

From a distance, Timothy's progress is barely visible, and he inches across the landscape, as though he is swimming alone in a wide featureless ocean with no sense of scale against which to measure the distance he gains.

Ethan is overwhelmed by the desire to shout out across the water to him, to warn him off, though he knows the distance between them is too far, and he wonders whether all hunters feel this impulse when they see their quarry. He watches until Timothy disappears where the road dips down, and though he

waits and continues to stare at the coast, he does not see him
again, and it occurs to Ethan that he has fabricated this event,
that he has been out on the water too long to tell the difference
between fantasy and reality.

# 5

# Timothy

O N   H I S   R E T U R N, Timothy's thoughts are all renewal and progress.

When he arrives back from his run, he stands between the house and the car, which he had parked two hours earlier. Not wanting to disrupt his new enthusiasm, he goes in at the passenger door and changes back into warmer clothes, then looks out through the windscreen at the kitchen door. He is not ready to go back into the house yet. Instead, he walks slowly down through the village to the row of houses where he remembers he and Lauren had stayed. They had decided on their destination by moving their fingers together over the map, his hand laid over hers, as they skimmed their fingertips across the coast until they found a place with a name that pleased them, a place where they could spend the time together just being themselves. He cannot now remember the name of the hotel in which they stayed, though the rudeness of their host is still fresh to him, as is the way in which he ushered them out of the bar area as soon as they arrived.

*'No room here,' the landlord says as they enter, loud enough to stop the conversations going on across the room and for all eyes to turn towards them. They wonder whether they have got the wrong place. They freeze on the threshold, half in and half out of the bar, with their two bags slung between them, and the landlord waves them away and goes back to wiping*

the bar down with a cloth, eyeing them from beneath thick eyebrows.

Outside, they are getting back into the car when they see the landlord appear again from a fire exit at the side of the building. He waves them over and when they do not come straight away he hisses something at them and waves again, this time with more urgency.

'Come on. Quick. Can't let them in there know I've got rooms empty. I've told them there are none free,' he says. He stares at their mud-spattered clothes with open disgust as they approach across the car park.

'That's okay, it's obvious there's a mistake,' says Lauren.

'No. No mistake. You just come in this way. I'll leave this door propped open and you can come and go through here. It's forty up front now and ten more if you want breakfast tomorrow.'

He leads them through the side door into a dimly lit hallway and they stand together awkwardly cramped in the small corridor as Timothy fumbles in his pockets for the money. Timothy has the vague suspicion they are being mugged and that they will be ejected from the side door the moment he has handed over the cash. There is a door tiled with small panels of obscured glass a little way into the corridor which leads through to the bar area and the landlord pushes them past this and to the foot of a flight of stairs.

'It's up there, top of the stairs. Walk quiet, mind.'

Lauren and Timothy exchange glances, but they are too tired to argue and they have handed over their money now. From what they had seen of the village as they drove in earlier that day, they are going to struggle to find a room anywhere else. They start up the stairs and the landlord follows closely behind. At the top he gives them a key, attached to a heavy and oversized wooden key fob.

'You'll find everything you need in there.' He points to the furthest left of four doors which lead off the landing ahead. 'That one's yours. Bathroom's through the door on the right. Don't worry about the other two, they're mine. Don't make too much noise on the floor. Them down there can't know you're here. Breakfast's at six and you'll need to be gone by nine.'

He turns to go and halfway down the staircase turns and hisses back up, 'And use the side door.'

'Can we come down for supper?' Lauren asks.

The landlord comes part way up the stairs towards them.

'I've already told you, steer clear of the bar, we're closed for food. You'll find no food here, not this time of the evening. I told you, I don't want you causing trouble.'

And with that he is heading back downstairs. Timothy wants to follow the landlord and hand the key back to him, but he has already turned the corner through the glass door and they decide going into the bar would be a bad idea.

At Lauren's insistence they jam a chair under the door handle when they turn in to sleep. It is dark outside now and there is nowhere else for them to go. As Timothy opens their bags, Lauren walks around the room and touches all the curtains in turn, the bedspreads, the lampshade on the bedside table that sits between the two single beds. All share the same pink floral pattern, a pattern that clashes with the garish swirls of the orangey-brown carpet. They lift out the side table and lamp and push the two beds together, trying not to make noise for fear they will bring the landlord back up the stairs. Lauren arranges the single duvets so they will cover both of them.

Above the beds, a small, gaudy painting of the Virgin Mary, all blues and golds, stares down at them with sad eyes from beneath her oversized crown. The paint is peeling from the picture and the face of the child she carries is obscured. Timothy and Lauren kick off their shoes and climb into bed still fully dressed beneath the textured nylon sheets. They laugh beneath the floral covers at *the strangeness of the place and listen to the dull sea of chatter from the bar beneath.*

*The next morning, they wait to be served breakfast in the empty bar area surrounded by the dark wood tables off which shines a harsh morning light.*

*'Could you do me two poached eggs on brown toast?' Lauren asks the barmaid, who looks to be about sixteen. The girl stands in between them and the window out onto the road, which throws her into a harsh silhouette.*

*'We don't have brown bread, just white. And we don't have poached eggs. We've got scrambled or fried.'*

*They wait until the girl has left the room to laugh, though they cannot be sure she has not heard them. When their breakfasts arrive, both Timothy and Lauren leave them untouched. The food sits, surrounded by a halo of grease, on plates that have been washed too many times to serve food anyone would want to eat. When Timothy returns from his morning run, he finds Lauren has once again blocked the bedroom door with a chair and he waits as she gets out of bed and pulls on a t-shirt to let him in. Keeping the game going, he steps inside and replaces the chair. They are trespassers in a strange place.*

Timothy walks along the street twice before he realises the hotel is no more. He finds the building from the screw points where the sign had been affixed to the wall, and it looks to him now as though it has been split into two, maybe three houses. There are more doors and windows than there had been, clumsily punched through the old walls. Through one of the windows he sees there are still tables and chairs in a room too large for a house and he figures there is still a pub here, though there is no real sign of that from the outside.

He winds his way down the two further tight rows of houses that separate this street from the sea, and finds himself passing a café that fronts onto the beach. Three men sit at a table in front of the closed café door, talking to another three who are making repairs to a trawl net spread out before them on the concrete walkway. The men continue their conversation as he approaches, though they all turn to watch him walk past. Timothy walks away and, rather than retrace his steps past the café to the metal staircase, he sits on the edge of the walkway and lets himself down onto the stones. The distance to the beach is further than it looked from the top and, half-falling, half-scrambling down the sloped sea wall, he lands awkwardly and looks around to see if anyone has noticed. The men repairing their nets are still watching him and he hears raised voices from the men at the café tables, though he cannot see them from where he is now standing on the beach.

Further down, a man in his late fifties or early sixties sits outside the stone building on the edge of the beach and Timothy approaches him. The man wears a pair of faded yellow waders, a thin jumper and a woollen cap. He is smoking. By the scattering of cigarette butts that fills the spaces in between the stones around the shack it seems he smokes often. He is feeding the edge of a net through his hands and cutting out knots with a stubby knife and his eyes are fixed on the gap in the cliff walls, looking out to the small patch of open water it reveals.

'You're the one took on Perran's place then,' he says, without turning towards Timothy.

It's a statement rather than a question, and one that echoes the steady animosity he felt in the stares of the men by the café, and the others he has received from the few people he has passed in the street since he arrived.

'Shorter than I thought you'd be, the way they talk about you down here.'

Timothy frowns and looks to see the man is smiling to himself though he maintains his gaze towards the sea.

'They love a story here. Love a story,' the man says. 'You

didn't expect a welcome party, did you? Know how they feel about incomers. Oh, they'll stop staring eventually. When they forget there was a time you weren't here. Not likely to happen anytime soon given what happened to Perran and you moving in there. It's not a thing they'll easy forget.'

There is a pause and Timothy thinks he has been dismissed. He makes to move away.

'Their memories aren't as long as they think. You get stuck in and they'll forget you, give it a few years. Other way they'd forget you is by getting yourself back up country. That'd work too.'

Timothy cannot think of what to say in response, and when he speaks, it is with a voice he does not recognise as his own, as though he has acquired a new accent since he has arrived here, one he was unaware he has developed.

'Perran?' he asks.

The older man shakes his head. It's not time for stories now obviously. Timothy changes tack.

'You look as though you're waiting for someone. I thought all the boats were usually back in by now,' he says. Watching for the boats has become a routine for Timothy, watching from the empty front bedroom of the house.

'Another thing you might be held responsible for, you're not careful,' the older man says. 'Got crews that don't want to fish. Most of them have been no further afield than the pub the last few weeks. Only one of them out at the moment and he's not fishing, just using up fuel, I reckon.'

Timothy starts to head down the beach.

'Clem,' the older man says before Timothy goes out of earshot. 'And the man you've got spooked, that'd be Ethan. I reckon you owe it to me to get him back on track, trouble it's causing me.'

The tide is low. Timothy walks down the beach as far as the

shoreline and the dark band of seaweed, driftwood and plastic shrapnel that marks the boundary between land and sea. There is no such distinction between sea and sky and the only marker he can find of the horizon are the container ships, which sit still, pictures hung on a featureless wall.

At the edge of the beach, Timothy makes his way out of the cove on the rocks and round to the right, mindful this time of the tide. He does not know why it surprises him that he cannot now find the rock on which he and Lauren had clung to each other ten years previously. The memory he holds is clear, unequivocal, and he now considers for a moment he has created an elaborate fiction of this event, that it never took place, at least not in the way he believes it did. Eventually, among the jutting, knife-edge rocks he finds a slab, smoother and flatter than the others, and sits on it looking out to sea, though he is still shaken slightly by the thought this may not be the same sea he and Lauren looked out on ten years previously.

He does not know how long he has been considering this thought, sitting on the flat rock, when he becomes aware of the boat, limping its way back towards the cove entrance. It is close in to the shore, close enough for him to see detail and to hear the engine spitting and hacking. He can see he has been spotted too, and the man on-board watches him openly, rudely even, through the small window of the wheelhouse. Timothy finds he cannot look away and stares back. He raises a hand, but the man on the boat does not return the gesture, and continues to stare at him until the boat passes out of sight as it enters the cove. Clem's words return to him, something about a debt he owes, some effect he's had on some fisherman he has never met, a slight for which he must atone, for which he has already been found guilty.

The tide has turned and Timothy turns his eyes away from the faint off-white wake left by the boat, dispersing slowly in the calm sea. He scrambles back around the shoreline and down the rocks onto the beach again, and sees Clem is unhitching the boat he had seen making its way back in. Clem sees him walking up the beach towards the hard standing and Timothy raises a hand, though Clem has already turned away from both the boat and from him and is climbing the metal staircase up towards the coast road.

He moves in close enough to read the boat's name painted on the transom. From a distance the *Great Hope* had looked like a boat from a picture postcard, all bright blues and whites. Up close it is ragged and the paint is peeling in thick strips from the cabin roof and walls, but she shows her age most below the waterline, where the scars of a life spent being dragged across the stones run deep in the thick metal hull. Timothy walks round the stern, to where a man in waders is hauling a net over the side of the boat onto the concrete.

'Give you a hand?' he calls up. 'You must be Ethan.'

Ethan stops, with half the net overboard, and stares down with an expression Timothy does not recognise. It is not animosity or anger. Fear maybe, and something else, which if he had to put a name to it might come out as hunger, though he knows as it crosses his mind it is not the right word.

'I'd like to see the village from out there sometime,' Timothy says, pointing out towards the sea. 'If you're ever short handed, you know, I could . . .'

'You shouldn't swim out there,' Ethan cuts him short. 'Not if you like breathing.'

Timothy flinches and looks around, hoping Ethan is talking not to him, but to someone else he has not yet noticed.

'I wasn't,' he starts to reply, and Ethan waves a hand, dismissing whatever it is he is about to say.

'I saw you swimming a mile out over there a couple of weeks back. You're green if you reckon on swimming in these waters.

42

The tide'll have you off those rocks before you know it and we'll be fishing you out a few days later or picking what's left of you off the beach. After she's had her way with you.'

Ethan waves the same hand back out in the direction of the sea.

'And if the tide doesn't get you, the chems will. You want to stay healthy past forty, alive past fifty, you'll remember to stay well out of the water.'

Timothy opens his mouth to respond, but Ethan has lowered his gaze back to the deck and returned to his work on the boat, and it seems clear to Timothy the conversation is over.

As he passes back towards the village, Timothy sees someone has hung, over the railings between the beach and the road, a row of jellyfish that are drying in the cold breeze, tattered and dirty, like snow that's been walked over too many times.

*'We ought to move down there. Let's do it. Now, before it's too late.'*

*Lauren laughs and throws a tea towel across the tiny kitchen, from where she is washing dishes, towards Timothy, who is sitting on the only worktop, finishing the glass of red wine she has left there. Timothy catches the tea towel and gives it a puzzled look before setting it down next to him by the hob.*

*'Before we get entrenched. You know. Before this place gets its claws into us. Just think of the place we'd be able to afford down there.'*

*'With whose money, mister? And anyway, it wasn't all post-card stuff, there was something weird about it,' Lauren replies and nods towards the towel he has set down and again towards the plates on the draining board. 'I see my subtle hint failed again. Pick that up and give me a hand.'*

*Timothy balances Lauren's glass on the tips of one of the stove's four-pronged burners and jumps down from the worktop. He drapes the towel over his shoulder, walks up* behind Lauren, puts his hands around her waist and kisses her neck.

'And no distractions either. Not until we've finished in here. You. Tea towel. Draining board. Full concentration. Now.'

Timothy feigns a look of reproach and picks up a plate from the crowded draining board. By the harsh light thrown by the bare bulb in the tiny kitchen Lauren is striking, and her neat bobbed hair throws dark shadows on her pale cheeks.

'And what, right now? Just because you like a place we've been doesn't mean we should move there. I've still got the rest of the year to go, and if you think Morgan will let his prize cow go without putting up a fight I think you're naïve,' Lauren says, and hands him a bundle of cutlery dripping water and soap bubbles, which he receives onto the tea towel in both hands.

'Morgan can screw himself,' he says without conviction. Lauren is right. He has held the job at Morgan's for just under a year, and to throw it away now would be foolish even by his standards. A rising star of the profession, or so Morgan tells him whenever he comes back with a new contract signed and sealed, or another client waiting with his chequebook open and his pen poised.

'Umm, hmm?'

Lauren flicks soap bubbles up at him and he flicks back with the tea towel. After putting her wet hands up in a motion of mock defeat, she pushes him gently backwards through the door into the sitting room of their new flat. He lets himself be overbalanced back onto the sofa, and pulls her with him.

Afterwards, he reaches up and takes a throw from the back of the sofa and lays it over the two of them. Lauren is on the brink of sleep, her head balanced on his chest, and Timothy listens in the darkness to the sounds of the city as they rise up from the streets and in through the window.

Some hours later, Lauren slides off the sofa and Timothy watches her stretch as though he is not there at all, and then *she silently picks up the clothes from the floor and chooses some more to wear for the day from the wardrobe that stands in the corner of the room. He watches her half-silhouetted as she dresses in that economical way she does and he marvels at the way her body fits into the thin woollen sweater she puts on. When she is gone, he rises from the sofa and transfers himself to the bed, taking the journey of four feet they had not managed to make the night before.*

*Sometime later in the morning, Lauren returns from her lectures and climbs into bed with him. The snow is thick on the pavements and roofs outside and they spend the rest of the day under the thick covers. At some point between the waking and sleeping as the afternoon wears itself out, she pulls him over onto his side so their foreheads and the tips of their noses touch and stares into his eyes and they stay like this for what may be minutes, but may also be hours.*

# 6

# *Timothy*

T IMOTHY IS STANDING on the deck of a vast ship, an expanse of thickly painted deck, as wide as a football pitch or wider. No birds perch or roost on the railings, though there are gulls wheeling far above in the white sky. He walks across the deck to the side facing the shore and can see the shape of the coast, unfamiliar from this angle. There are fields marked out by their boundaries and clumps of trees, and he wonders whether it is the distance that keeps him from seeing any sheep or cattle grazing. At this distance, the entrance to the cove is hidden from him and blends into the landscape, but he thinks he can see the village rising up the steep hillside, and above it the white beacon on top of the hill. This is the only sign there is life here, other than the sea road that follows the contours of the coast as far as he can see in one direction and that comes to an end at the far side of the village. Beyond the village, the landscape is indistinct.

To his left, though far off, rising up from the deck of the ship there is a tower, sombre and tall and featureless aside from the broad expanse of glass that obscures the bridge, where the captain and crew would have looked down, over their cargo. The reflective glass stretches all round this tower, so the captain would have seen, too, the broad curving route he ploughed through the sea, though now the boat is stationary, fixed in place. He can feel the massive engines far beneath him, inert and cold.

There is no movement from the tower and no noise other than the wind in his ears and the screaming of the gulls overhead. The gulls turn in wide arcs above him and take turns to dive down towards him, warning him off, warning him to stay clear, though as far as he can see, there is no way off the ship.

The huge plate-glass windows of the bridge reflect the grey sky and Timothy has a strong sensation, though there is no sign of anyone else there, that he is being observed dispassionately, of something or someone behind the glass looking down onto this tiny figure far below on the deck. He feels there could be someone, or a bank of someones, standing behind the glass watching to see what he will do next, with clipboards lowered, making notes on his progress or lack thereof. Or maybe it is the blank gaze of someone or something still asleep, something passive that he should not disturb. The intensity of this feeling grows as he stares up at the tower, and with the gulls diving closer with each pass, he looks around for shelter, but there is no hiding place.

The offshore wind is cold and there is no protection from it on the exposed deck. He does not feel like moving towards the tower despite the shelter it might offer from the wind biting at his face. From where he stands, leant against the railings, he sees, between the ship and the land, small boats circling, like fish in a glass bowl and he has the sense if he threw something, anything, down into the water below, they would turn towards him, to the disturbance in the water. The sensation that he is looking in on something is overwhelming.

Timothy is suddenly anxious about what lies beyond the ship in the other direction, of what he will be able to see from this platform from the other side of the deck that faces out, away from the land. He has a strong feeling there will be nothing there when he gets to the other side, no horizon to see, no waves, no features at all, that this boat represents the very edge of something. He turns from the railings and starts to walk across the huge deck to the other side and, as the sense of anxiety increases, the walk becomes a run. He trips several times over hatches and iron rings anchored into the deck on his way across and beneath him he can feel the gaping emptiness of the cargo holds and beneath that the emptiness of the sea. When he reaches the guard rail and looks out over the other side, he breathes again, relieved to see, far below him, waves that are evidence the sea continues beyond, though when he follows the scene up from the point where the ship's hull meets the water, he finds he cannot distinguish between the sea and the sky, and the empty expanse feels oppressive and close.

Timothy wakes and, for a few moments in the darkness, he wonders whether he is still aboard the ship, somewhere deep within its hold, and he lies still and waits for some sensation of the boat moving on the water beneath him. The feeling of oppression stays with him and he cannot shake the sensation that the boundary marked out by the container ships is important somehow.

Timothy has been here several weeks now and he wonders sometimes whether he is causing more damage to the house than he is improving it. He coughs. It is a cough he has developed from the clouds of plaster that sit heavy in all the rooms, dust that has found its way into his lungs and beneath his fingernails and eyelids. The feeling of oppression, he realises, had been there before his dream. His throat is dry and he feels the house pressing down on him.

To shake off the feeling, he gets out of bed and walks down the staircase, running his hands along the wooden struts of the walls. They are the thin ribs of the house, exposed as he has peeled back layers of wallpaper and then crumbling plaster from the walls. He heads for the kitchen, pours himself a glass of water from the sink and sees someone has slid an envelope beneath the back door and it stands out white against the slate floor. Ethan has reconsidered the offer he made weeks before and they are to sail the following morning. He looks at the clock on the kitchen wall and sees it is just gone four in the morning. Too early to continue his work on the house and too late to return to sleep. In any case he cannot face returning to the dream he has just left, and instead he puts on his running clothes and walks out to stretch in the darkness that will last another hour yet at least. As he leaves, he tucks his phone into the pocket in the back of his running shorts. He will call Lauren later, when he can get reception. He runs out into the dark and the mist of the early morning. Lauren will still be asleep, warm and ensconced in duvet. There is still some way to go before he can call for her to join him. He will not tell her his worries for the task that is still ahead, or the scale of the work that still faces him in the house, nor that it feels to him in some way like a thin soil that crumbles between his fingers as he touches it.

On his run out of the village, he takes a detour past the beach. There is a light on in the cabin of one of the boats and by it he sees Ethan's jacketed torso haloed on the deck of the *Great Hope*. Ethan's head is down, his face hidden in the dark shadow of a cap as he works at something on deck. Timothy thinks about approaching him and asking him again about the line of container ships and whether they can pass out that way when they head out. But already the dream is losing its intensity and he is sure by the time it is light he will have shaken whatever it is that is pulling him out to them. Ethan is absorbed in his task and the sound of the waves on the beach means Timothy would have to shout above it to get his attention. He will ask Ethan about it later perhaps.

# 7

# *Ethan*

'WHAT'S OUT THERE?'
This is the evening before they are due to sail,
when they stand on the deck of the grounded boat and Ethan
talks Timothy through what they will be doing the next
day.

'Out there? You mean in the water?' Ethan replies. 'What's
left when there's nothing worth catching. Dogfish. Jellyfish.
Dead things or dying things you wouldn't put a fork to.'

'Why do you, then . . . ?' Timothy starts to ask, but changes
tack. 'No, beyond the ships. Why do you stay this side of them?
Is it a safety thing?'

Ethan, backed into a corner, can think of nothing to say in
reply and, instead, goes back to running the edge of the net
along the palm of his hand. Checking the nets usually calms
him, but now his thoughts are out on the water, out beyond
the line of ships.

In the sky's gradual lightening before dawn, half an hour or so
after they have passed out from the protection of the rocks at
the mouth of the cove, Ethan steers the boat on a heading away
from the rest of the fleet and mutes the radio. The morning
air is calm and the dark sky above them shifts from a band of
darkest blue to a light yellow and then to a deep orange on the
horizon. The outlines of the container ships are silhouetted in
the darkest band of orange, where it starts to gradate back to
the deepest blue of the sea below.

Ethan observes from the small cabin of the *Great Hope* as Timothy stands on the foredeck trying to find his legs. He has not said a word to the newcomer since they cast off, and Timothy looks unsure as to whether he should stand or sit, and he settles for an uncomfortable position somewhere between the two, with his leg braced against the side of the boat, one hand gripping the guard rail hard, his knuckles white and the rest of his hand pale already in the freezing sea air. Timothy is about Perran's height, though he has none of the same thinness around the neck and face, nor the same thick head of hair, but for all the differences between the two, they might be related. Something in the way he holds himself perhaps, or something in his eyes. Ethan checks their heading again, makes some adjustments and tries to shake off this transplanting of Perran onto the newcomer.

As they head out towards the ships, he concentrates on the spaces in between them, and tries, unsuccessfully, to block them out of his mind. After an hour or so, in which the ships grow in stature, at first steadily and then with increasing speed, they come up close alongside one, as though it has drawn the smaller vessel in, the larger body exerting its own gravity. The ship looks as though it is rooted straight down into the seabed for all it moves in the water. It looks to be a fixed point, as steady and solid as any of the houses in the village. Ethan has never sailed this close to the sentinels, let alone passed between them to the other side. Until recently he has never even thought of going out between them, not since the ships arrived a little short of ten years ago.

*First the letters, then the ships.*

*Letters from the department start to arrive shortly after Perran's death, edicts and instructions for the new fishing grounds worded in archaic and obscure language. It is left to Clem to interpret these missives, and he reads them aloud to the fleet as* they congregate on the beach, and then he tacks each of the letters to the noticeboard in the winch house.

'Pursuant to the department's previous notification of the revised fishing grounds, boundaries will be marked for the purpose of controlling fish stocks in restricted zones and for the containment and management of harmful waterborne agents,' Clem reads.

Clem is standing on the step outside the winch house, a head higher than the other fishermen. Looking at him brings to mind a sepia photograph Ethan has seen in a frame on the wall of the winch house beside the noticeboard. The photograph shows a stern priest standing alone on the beach as the boats cast off. The priest wears full canonical robes and holds in one hand a chain and censer that is leaking smoke. He is swinging the censer out in front of him with one hand and the other is raised to the departing fleet in a gesture of benediction. Ethan has always felt sorry for this man in the photograph, standing alone on the grey stones, looking out of place.

'Motorised and sail-driven vessels, of classes one to four inclusive, are not to be permitted to come within 500 feet of boundary markers, and owners of vessels straying into the restricted zone will be subject to prosecution under the following Acts . . .'

Ethan has stopped listening to Clem and instead turns to look for the reaction of the other skippers and crews around him. They are, as usual, silent for the most part, though some are talking beneath their breath, or kicking the stones under their boots. One or two have already started to walk away from the beach.

When Clem has stopped talking, Ethan looks around and sees some of the older skippers shaking their heads in disgust or shame. He watches one, a fisherman who has been sailing out of the cove as long as any of the others there, as he walks off the beach and throws his son the keys to his boat, before he retreats to his house for good.

*That morning no one sails out of the cove. And over the course of the next few days a few of the skippers go down to their boats, strip them of anything useful or valuable and retire to their houses, leaving their boats to rot on the shore. For some this news is more than they are prepared to take, with the fish stocks falling fast and the prices so low.*

*Overnight the ships arrive and are anchored at regular intervals along the horizon. After a few days, Ethan wonders whether the ships might always have been there, unnoticed and waiting for their chance to edge closer towards the shore, into sight.*

The letters, still tacked up on the noticeboard, are now speckled all over with mould. The ink on them has faded and they hold less power somehow in the face of Timothy's questions. And having Timothy on board, Ethan finds, gives him a sense of confidence, a sense of having been dared and of not wanting to lose face.

As Ethan steers a course between the ships, his feeling of unease grows. With the sun still low on the horizon, the small fishing boat comes into the field of a long shadow cast across the water by the ship's derrick. The *Great Hope* passes closer to the hulking mass than he had intended, as if the smaller boat is being drawn in towards it. The water around the boat is still and darker for the mass that lies beneath it and the ship's hull rises sheer and steep, dwarfing the smaller boat. The lower half of the ship's visible hull is painted red and is stained with patches of rust, and at the waterline he sees the sea is oil slicked and contaminated. Above, the upper part of the hull is painted a dark grey, and the derrick and uppermost part of the deck are white, or were at some time. Rust shows through the white paint even from a distance, and as they get closer they see long scars drawn into the paintwork. On the side of the ship, what is presumably its name is written in letters ten feet tall or taller, though it is written in a script Ethan does not understand. The letters look familiar, as though he should be able to read them, though each is transfigured and mutated, and though they pass close to the ship, the letters do not resolve themselves into anything that carries meaning he can decipher. Deeper into the boat's shadow, he sees signs riveted onto the hull at intervals. They are warnings perhaps, or impart vital information, though they are all written in the same familiar, but unreadable, script.

Ethan knows that the other three crews will be watching their passage through binoculars from their cabins, and almost certainly discussing his diversion over the radio. 'Ethan's lost it again' will almost certainly be the topic of conversation. Tomas will be the most vocal on this subject, as the group's malcontent, as the one who has threatened over and again to leave. Rab will be shouting Tomas down as he always has done, saying Ethan should do what the hell he wants. And Jory will be peacekeeping and keeping whatever opinions he holds to himself.

Though he has never seen so much as a single light on within any of them since the day they arrived, Ethan half-expects to be hailed by one of the ships, to hear a siren or a horn blast, warning them to turn back, or for floodlights to fire up. He drops the boat speed to reduce the noise they make as they pass beneath the ship's high walls, but there is no warning or any sign at all they have been seen, just the sound of a colony of gulls that must roost on the sills of the ship's windows and doorways. From the sound of it the colony is a large one, and the birds' shrieks have grown louder the closer to the ship they have come. Disturbed by the boat, a host of the birds lifts up from the deck far above them. After their initial dispersal into the sky, the birds start to congregate above the boat, so that, between the high walls of the ship to one side and the flock above them the morning light is reduced to a kind of dusk. A few of the larger birds make circles around the *Great Hope*, and they spiral down towards the small boat in uneven loops. As the birds grow bolder, flying down to within metres of them, Ethan sees Timothy edge around the side of the cabin until he is in its shelter. The noise of the shrieking gulls becomes unbearable for a few minutes, and the birds become a heavy cloud which sits just metres above the boat. Timothy, looking nervous and apologetic, moves into the tiny wheelhouse until the number of birds above them starts to thin out, and they back off from their diving attacks. Many of the birds follow the *Great Hope* when it clears the ship, as though they are seeing off an intruder, but they too lose interest as the boat makes its way further out. When Ethan opens up the engine again, the few birds still following turn back towards the container ship. After a while the gaps between the ships close in again behind them and half an hour later Ethan cuts back the engine and emerges from the cabin.

'What happens now?' Timothy shouts back down the deck towards him. 'It wasn't so hard, was it? No one opened fire on us. No monster waiting for us on this side. No chasm opened up, dragging us down to the depths.'

Timothy's voice sounds odd and out of place as it breaks the silence and Ethan can see speaking has made him uneasy. Up until this point Timothy has been silent, following Ethan's lead, and Ethan does not tell him they have both broken rules now.

Ethan moves towards Timothy so he does not have to raise his voice against the wind.

'What happens now is we lower the nets, wait a while, pull them up. Then we lower them back down and pull them up a few more times and then when we're tired we go home. If we're lucky we'll take back a few dogfish for our trouble.'

Ethan too, though, is looking around to see what difference if any there is between where they were before and where they are now.

'If we get bored, we pull the nets early and go move some

55

lobster pots around by the cove,' he continues. 'Not that the pots deserve the title. Empty nets. Empty pots.'

They fall back into silence, until Ethan has to talk Timothy through lowering the net, and when he does speak, he surprises himself with the kindness of tone he uses. Timothy starts to lower the gear, and Ethan can see him, as clear as anything, catch a hand or a sleeve in the netting and pull himself over the side, as clear as he can see the man standing on deck before him. He pushes Timothy to one side and takes control until the nets are in the water. He's doing better than some of the local boys Ethan has taken out on the *Great Hope* before. He's not crouching in a corner puking his guts into a bucket, and that's something when the swell is long and slow as it is now they have moved out from the still water around the ships.

Ethan lowers the largest of the nets, a long gillnet he uses when the boats aren't in close quarters, and while they wait, both men look out towards a horizon that is not punctuated by the presence of the container ships. As he looks out across the ocean, Ethan has a sudden sense of vertigo, and not just an awareness of the distance below the two men down to the sea bed, but horizontally too, as though, if the world tipped, there would be nothing to stop them falling for as far as they could fall, and he brings his gaze back into the boat. Timothy observes the silence and Ethan observes Timothy and tries not to see Perran in him. Despite Ethan's earlier suggestion, they stay out on the water throughout the short day and way on into the evening, and neither man questions the other, as though they are each pushing the other on.

It is the early hours of the next morning when Ethan first catches sight of the shoal, lit by the moon in a cloudless sky. The fish appear at first as a lightening of the sea beneath the boat as of a cloud scudding beneath the waves, their scales catching the moonlight. Ethan is leaning on the gunwale smoking and he nudges Timothy with the toe of his boot, to raise him from where he has fallen asleep leant against the wall of the cabin. The shoal is broad and moving fast, close to the surface, and Ethan works quickly to bring the boat round to face it as the fish pass beneath the boat.

The net, when they raise it, comes up heavy with pale bodies and both men work hard at getting the catch onto the deck. The fish they pull are colourless and long, and their scales, when Ethan lifts some of them with his knife, are translucent. Ethan holds one of the fish up and he sees its eyes are pale too, as though it does not see and has never seen, and it is dull and lifeless, though it has been less than a minute since they raised the net. Beneath the skin, the outlines of organs are visible, shadows in the pale flesh. As he picks up more of the fish, he sees, in some of them, that thick bunches of roe show through the distended skin of their underbellies.

The two men process the fish into crates, handling each one gently. When they are finished, they stand at the open hatch, looking down into the hold at the catch.

Ethan drops the net a second time and again it comes up full, and of the same fish, and the two men work until the hold is heavy with bodies. When they have finished, Ethan stares down again through the hatch. The fish in boxes laid one on top of the other remind him of the silver fish of his dream, though these are calm and still in the bottom of the boat.

Ethan does not call it in immediately. But when he does, the radio lights up.

'You've been in for more luck then? Dogfish again?'

The sound of Clem's voice across the radio sounds harsh in the confines of the small cabin.

'No. They're . . . well, I don't know for sure. None like I've seen before,' Ethan replies. 'There's plenty of them though. More of any fish than I've seen before.'

As Ethan describes the fish to Clem, he watches Timothy walking back out onto the deck and opening up the hatch door to look down on the catch. Ethan finds he is willing the man to cover up the hold and to step away from the hatch. He is only half-listening to Clem on the radio as he watches Timothy through the scratched window, and he lets the wheel go while he rolls a cigarette on the dashboard in front of him.

'There's rumours you've been fishing off grid,' Clem is saying over the radio. 'If you have, I don't care and, moreover, I don't want to know about it. Just get yourself back in and get that catch in with you. I'll have buyers here by the time you're back.'

Clem signs off the radio and Ethan calls out from the cabin for Timothy to take the wheel. Timothy looks bewildered and Ethan points towards the shore.

'See that marker on the hill, point her at that and we won't go wrong.'

He knows it is not a fair thing to say. There's no way Timothy can see the marker on the distant land, which is a uniformity of greens in the distance, but Timothy nods uncertainly and looks towards the line Ethan has indicated. In the early morning light, as they draw close to them, the ships loom large again, and Timothy steers a course that keeps the container ships an equal distance on either side this time. Even so, as the boat passes between them, Ethan hears the sound of the gulls rise in a great crescendo, and he sees them take flight from the ship they had passed close to earlier. The noise of the birds starts to cover even that of the engine and a huge flock follows the *Great Hope* in towards the shore.

For much of the return journey Ethan wedges himself in the wheelhouse doorway, talking on the radio and taking more questions from Clem and the other skippers, though none of them makes any further mention of the *Great Hope*'s excursion beyond the ships. Between bursts of activity on the radio he looks over towards Timothy at the wheel and feels a new sensation, one he can't explain to himself.

By the time they make the shore, there is a line of vans along the sea road and a crowd is waiting for them on the beach. Ethan finds he is scanning the figures gathered on the shore and even before he sees the woman in the grey coat, standing on the outskirts, he knows she is going to be there. As the boat nears the shore her eyes burn holes in the bow, or perhaps, he thinks, she is looking towards him, and he lowers his eyes to avoid her gaze.

# 8

## *Timothy*

F ROM WHERE HE stands on the deck of the *Great Hope*,
Timothy can see a small crowd standing on the beach, dis-
turbing the uniformity of the grey stones, as the boat turns into
the mouth of the cove. He looks back to see whether Ethan has
noticed, but the sun, which has just crested the horizon, sits
low on the line and reflects off the windows of the cabin and
he can see nothing of the other man. Timothy returns his gaze
to the shore. The coast road, usually as empty as the beach,
is crowded too, with cars and vans, and it looks as though a
travelling market has made camp in the village.

The noise from the people gathered on the beach takes over
from the retch of the boat as Ethan cuts the engine and they
drift the final few feet to the shore. He can hear raised voices,
aggressive and demanding, and as the noise resolves itself into
individual voices, he understands several men and women on the
shore are shouting each other down, arguing over the catch they
are bringing back in. As they draw in, the large bulk of Clem
pushes through the crowd and the people on the beach fall back.
The arguments continue behind him, though in lowered tones.

Clem waits for him to come forward on the deck, winch
cable in hand, and he throws it up for Timothy to secure to
the thick loop of rope. The metal block catches awkwardly on
Timothy's hand and he drops it and fumbles with the heavy
chain, unsure of what to do, and Ethan comes forward too and

takes it from him. Ethan looks nervous of the attention they are receiving and keeps his eyes lowered from the crowd on the beach, going through familiar actions to arrange the gear on the boat. Timothy finds again that he has no useful role to perform and he stands back while Ethan works on. Since they made their catch, neither man has spoken of it to the other, nor of anything else, and aside from the chatter from the radio, they have returned to the beach in a silence that seems to Timothy somehow less aggressive than the silence in which they left the beach.

After Clem pulls the *Great Hope* clear of the tide line, Timothy hears the winchman warn some of the men and women gathered on the beach to stand clear, and he brings a ladder to the side of the boat. Timothy lets himself down and then wonders whether he ought to return to help Ethan with whatever he is doing. After standing a moment at the foot of the ladder, Timothy decides to leave Ethan be. The other man is probably glad to have the space to himself again.

A group of men he recognises as crew from the other boats has gathered by the *Great Hope*, waiting to receive the boxes of fish as Ethan lowers them down. They push their way through the crowd and create a barrier between the boat and the men from the vans, who are moving in too, forming a semicircle around the vessel. The buyers remind Timothy of wolves in a pack, vying for the best position, closest to the kill. He wonders where they all came from and whether they are going to start pushing and shoving to get to the fish first as the pile of crates grows, but the fishermen's warning glances seem enough to hold them back, and they ignore the barrage of questions about the fish and their condition. A few of the men gathered fire questions at Timothy, though he is too dazed by the scene and the clamour to answer. When he does not answer immediately, they return to arguing among themselves and Timothy can hear money being discussed and the prices being pushed back and forward, and he sees Clem at the centre of it all, looking calmly on as the price rises.

Ethan is still standing on the deck and seems unsure of what to do next. He is looking out of the boat for something or someone. For a moment Timothy wonders if Ethan is looking for him, but his tiredness keeps him walking in the direction of the house he now refers to, even to himself, as Perran's.

Timothy is still unable to feel his hand from where he caught it on the cable block. He pushes his way through to the edge of the crowd and is glad when he has some space again for himself, to be away from the stares of the buyers and the villagers.

There is another person standing on the outskirts of the commotion on the beach, a woman he has seen before, dressed in a long, pale grey coat, as dissimilar to the grey of the stones on the beach as it is possible to be. She is looking out over the proceedings as though she is watching a play, at a distance and with detached amusement. As Timothy passes her, she raises her eyes to him and a fraction later she smiles a thin conspiratorial smile, a look that suggests they share something. The woman has grey eyes, paler even than her coat, and he is taken aback by them, more so than he is by the events of the past few hours. Her look is that of a lighthouse beam on a dark night that illuminates the sea around for a fraction of a second and then passes on, and the look they share is over almost as soon as it starts. The woman in grey returns her gaze to the men shouting down by the boat. Timothy continues his climb up the beach and a few yards further on turns back towards the scene. He sees two of the men in the crowd looking back up the beach towards the woman, and as they do she nods at them in affirmation or encouragement and they push their way forward through the small crowd towards Clem.

When Timothy looks back again as he reaches the road he

sees the deal has been concluded and now the crowd is split between those still interested in the fish in the crates coming out of the hold and those now dispersing. Some of them are staring up the beach towards the place where he stands. Clem and the crews of the fishing boats are now in this group, and he feels their gaze follow him as he makes his way up through the village.

Timothy reaches Perran's and falls into his bed fully clothed. He lies there for a while and a tiredness that is both physical and mental drapes itself over him like a thick blanket. He fights for a few minutes to stay awake and to recall all that has happened since he left the shore in the early morning, but it is like fighting an incoming tide and eventually he falls asleep and into a dream in which he is diving a long swan dive down from a high concrete platform into a clear sea. He passes down through the warm and cold streams of the sea's subtle strata, until the light that floods the surface gives way to darkness, until the unbearable pressure crushing down on him collapses his lungs and arteries, and he swims down further into the depths. Until the unbearable cold of the deep becomes warm again at the openings in the deepest flooded valleys. He dreams of the vents where life still clings on to the hydrothermal streams that escape the earth's core, of the shrimps, the crabs, the biosludge that survived the great oceanic apocalypse, and feels the heat of the vents sear the skin on his sunken face as he leans in closer to look. As he swims back towards the surface, his collapsed lungs burn and expand, and as the darkness and the pressure give way to light again, he swims through a lane of translucent fish, packed so close he has to fight his way through them, so close there is no longer water, just fish, packed closely, and he knows however hard he thrashes against them he will make no progress, and eventually, when his muscles give out, when his lungs stop their burning, he lets himself slip down into the mass of fish and the translucence becomes darkness and he dreams of nothing more until he wakes in a weak, fading afternoon light.

Sipping from a glass of water to ease his parched throat, Timothy leans forward against the cold bedroom window and looks down towards the beach. The crowds have dispersed and the vans are gone, but he can still hear noise from the beach, a celebration, and the sound of loud conversation and of glass clinking carried up to him in the early evening on-shore breeze. As the darkness grows he can hear a song or a shanty being sung, a drunken song to which they all know the words and which ebbs and flows on the wind, and the party continues. As he looks down through the village, with his head against the now clouded glass, Timothy has the feeling, that despite the closeness of the people in the houses below and those gathered on the beach, he is profoundly alone here.

Later, when he is in the kitchen fixing a meal, he hears a noise much closer to the house, from the darkness in the front garden. He feels exposed standing in the kitchen. The light from the single bare bulb above spills onto him, and the windowpanes frame squares of darkness and he can see nothing of the garden beyond. He searches through the toolbox, which has taken up permanent residence on the kitchen table, for a torch, and goes out into the garden, though by the time he is out of the house, the noise he heard has stopped and there are no sounds either from the village below. He sweeps the garden with the torch beam, walks down to the gate and finds, laid out on the top of the stone wall that borders the garden, a package wrapped loosely in paper. He unties the string wrapped round the parcel and finds, within, a neat stack of the fish he and Ethan had caught earlier that day. He looks at them for a while in the torchlight, lays the torch on the wall and picks one from the pile, gently with both hands. In the torch beam he sees the translucence of the scales has already started to turn milk white.

He looks at the small offering for a while and leaving the fish where they are, he returns to the house, and digs out from his toolbox a trowel, the only tool he has that will do the job. In the darkness, lit only by the light from his kitchen window and the torch, which he lays on the grass next to him, he digs a small grave for the fish beneath the tree furthest from the house, and buries them there, under the tattered streamers which hang from its branches.

# 9

# *Ethan*

E THAN HAD SPENT much of the money he made from the catch on drinks for the other crews who stayed on late into the night. He had paid off a few debts too, but he was aware, as he did so, of the other debt he owed. And whether it was to Perran or to Timothy to whom the offering should be made, he was still not sure. Perhaps it did not matter as long as he offered them up. After the party had died down and the villagers had dispersed and rolled their ways back up the hill to their houses, he had returned to the *Great Hope* to retrieve the fish he had held back.

It had seemed important at the time. Like it was the right thing to do, though the terms had been for all the fish, every one to come off the boat, the same as it was the first time. As part of the deal, one of the two men who accompanied the woman in grey had handed him a legal-looking document several pages long and asked him to sign, as soon as the other buyers had started to leave the beach. Ethan made a show of looking through the wad of papers, a document that seemed unsuited to the place it had ended up, too clean and delicate against the contrasting dirt and oil of the beach and the roughness of Ethan's hands. He recognised the insignia of the Department of Fisheries and Aquaculture on the cover sheet and as he skimmed through the papers the text swam before his eyes and he found he could not coerce what was written there to reconcile itself into words and sentences he could recognise. He had rubbed his eyes a few times, with no effect on the legibility of the document, but tiredness had won out and he had proffered the contract back to the man. The man pulled a pen from his suit pocket and handed it over, indicating, with its nib, a space on the last page. Ethan was surprised to see his name already printed there, and surprised too that there was at last something on the document he could read clearly. He pressed the document up against the hull of the *Great Hope* and signed it, soaking some of the pages on the other side with diesel and grime from the boat. When he handed the papers back, the second man stepped forward and took a roll of cash from his pocket. He handed it over to Clem, who pocketed his share before handing the rest over to Ethan. Ethan climbed up the ladder to unload the fish.

Standing waist deep in the hold and passing the crates up to Rab, who had climbed on board to help him, Ethan had removed a couple of the pale fish from each of the crates and placed them into the one of the empty boxes down in the shadow of the hold.

When all the crates were unloaded, he came up onto the deck and saw the grey woman was still staring down towards the *Great Hope* from the road. In the space between the boat and the woman in grey looking on, the two men in their suits looked incongruous carrying the crates of fish and they struggled with them on the stones, watched by the villagers.

As the last of the crates had made its way up to the van, the grey woman had exchanged words with the two men. One of them held his hands out away from his suit as though he was worried he would contaminate it. The other was leaning against the van and had the ankle of one of his legs resting above the knee of his other leg and was wiping his black shoes with a handkerchief he had pulled out from his suit pocket. All three were looking down towards the boat and towards Ethan. He wondered whether they were going to return to the beach and insist on inspecting the empty hold, but after a few raised words that carried across to him, they did not return to the boat. Ethan wondered whether she suspected he had held some back, and as he was clearing the boat, he threw some nets down over the box in which he had stored the fish for Timothy.

# *Timothy*

T IMOTHY IS SURPRISED when Ethan seeks him out a few days later and asks him if he will come out on the boat again. He considers it for a while. The house is disintegrating under his care and Lauren is due to arrive in less than a month.

That evening at sundown, he makes his way down to the shore, and he reaches the beach to find it busy again, this time with the crews preparing their boats, and a larger gathering than he has seen before amassed around them. As he passes between the boats that crowd the mid-tide beach, Timothy is aware of the sideways glances of those standing around. The earlier hostility he had felt is no longer there and it has been replaced by interest – intense interest and scrutiny. The villagers still avoid speaking to him as he walks by. His nods towards those whose eyes he catches are returned hurriedly, before each in turn averts their eyes.

Clem is the only person on the beach who speaks to him directly, and in a voice loud enough to be overheard.

'Problem for most of them is they have to pass the pub to get to their boats, and most times the pub wins out,' he says, and there is a volley of insults from the fishermen and laughter too, a sound Timothy realises he has not heard since he arrived in the village.

Clem then lowers his voice.

'All change now though. The haul you brought in last. Regular golden hen you are.'

Timothy stares at Clem, trying to figure out the meaning of this last statement, but Clem has already moved away, heading down the beach with a stack of crates, which he passes up to one of the boys standing on the deck of the nearest boat.

Timothy spots Ethan arranging crates of nets on the deck of the *Great Hope*, and he watches the fisherman as he organises the crates, like he is completing a puzzle to allow the two men room enough to walk on the crowded deck. When Ethan looks up and notices Timothy, he gestures to him to come up.

Timothy is unable to interpret the look Ethan gives him as he climbs aboard the *Great Hope*. It's the same look he saw on the other man's face as when they pulled up their catch of silver fish. He steps off the ladder onto the deck and has the feeling that in some way the *Great Hope* is, itself, a net of sorts and, somehow, that he is starting to become caught up in its folds. The afternoon is wearing itself out and the crews make ready to leave.

'Bremming tonight,' says Ethan, the first words he has spoken to Timothy since he came on board. 'Good sign.'

They leave the cove and, as they pass the rocks, Timothy understands what Ethan means. With the light fading fast, he sees, in the boat's wake, burning phosphorescence that dances just below the surface where the water has been disturbed. He watches it in the eddies and small currents caused by the boat's passing until it tails off, as the wake calms and the water becomes dark again. After a while, the darkness is punctuated only by the lights of the small fleet of fishing boats and the occasional brighter flash of a searchlight as one of the crew works on the foredeck. As they make their course over the water, these thin lights spread out from each other like the long fingers of a hand flexing. One of them Timothy loses in the darkness, and the others stay close to the *Great Hope*, and the lights of the small, silent waterborne community dance unsteadily on the sea's surface.

# 11

# Ethan

AFTER THE CATCH, no one, not even the other crews, had asked Ethan about his excursion beyond the container ships, as if they did not really want to know the answer. Their celebrations that night had been strained with all that was unsaid. No one wanted to talk about the fish themselves, though the catch warranted discussion, nor the circumstances in which they had come to be landed.

'Catch is a catch,' a few of them had said, and others around had nodded in agreement, as though that was all that needed to be said on the matter. Timothy, on the other hand, was discussed in detail. Ethan had noticed the stories about the newcomer had started to transform, to transfigure somehow into fictions of redemption, and the more beer that was drunk, the wilder the stories of his influence became. But of the *Great Hope* passing outside the fleet's boundary lines, Clem was the only one who came close to asking.

'Lucky catch,' he had said. This was after most of the others had gone home and the two men surveyed the beach that was littered with the cans and bottles of their impromptu party. 'Wouldn't want to interrogate it too closely though, for anyone's sake.'

Clem had stood up from his seat by the wheelhouse and pushed his hands into his jacket pocket, perhaps waiting for Ethan to comment or perhaps waiting for his words to sink in.

In place of an answer, Ethan had proffered Clem another beer from the crate by which he was sitting, and Clem had shaken his head and walked off up the beach, leaving Ethan alone in the dark, two hours before the sun threatened the horizon.

'Who was Perran?'

Timothy looks startled by the question that has slipped out, breaking the silence, and Ethan watches him as he wishes it back into his mouth. It is out though and contains, within it, an accusation that Timothy has been misled somehow.

The boat feels small now and Ethan's feelings of warmth towards Timothy compete with the feelings of guilt he drags up, with the acute anxiety Timothy brings on board with him. As they stand side by side on the deck, Ethan thinks how it would take only a few steps and a shove to tip the other man into the water, and how few questions would be asked of him later if that were to happen. They are a long way from shore and he is stronger than the incomer, he is sure of that, and more stable on his feet on the shifting deck.

Timothy has decided to return to silence, as though he sees the point of the rules now it suits him, as though the silence is fine with him after all. He is looking out of the boat, back towards the shore, his fingers fretting at the bare wood where the paint is peeling away.

'What will you gain by knowing?' Ethan asks finally, though whether he asks the question out of pity or despair, he is not sure.

He is unwilling to encourage Timothy, but it is clear to him Timothy now has nothing but the question burning out through his eyes, and the urge to push the incomer over the side comes back to Ethan stronger than before. He wonders whether Timothy even knows why he is asking, where the question came from, why it has taken hold of him.

The two men hold each other's gaze, until the boat slides down the face of a wave and both men lose their footing on the deck and stagger about, reaching for handholds. The sea is choppy now, the waves starting to build themselves up into a confusion of white horses, and the wind has picked up too. Timothy's knee, braced against the side of the boat, buckles. Ethan sees he does not anticipate the wave, which breaks over the side of the boat, and as Timothy scrabbles again for a handhold, Ethan looks away over the side of the boat, as Timothy falls down hard on his knees on the deck.

As they prepare to cast the nets, Ethan looks over at Timothy and wonders whether he is going to answer the question Ethan now wishes he had not asked. Ethan is aware of each sharper intake of breath from the other man, though he can't make out whether Timothy is trying to articulate an answer to the question himself, or is trying to withhold the question of his own that is fighting to resurface.

Later, after they have dropped the nets several times and the nets have come up empty, Ethan and Timothy stand on the side of the deck. It is Ethan who breaks their silence again.

'There's a midden behind the winch house on the beach, you know? In between the winch house and the wall. Have you seen it?'

Timothy shakes his head.

'Whelk shells. Masses of them. You ever eaten whelk?'

Timothy shakes his head again.

'Tastes like nothing, just grit,' Ethan says. 'There's folk here know hard times is all I'm saying. You understand?'

Timothy shakes his head. He is lost. Ethan stops talking for a while, rolls and lights a cigarette and the smoke whirls around their heads before it is lifted into a sky that is now heavy with rain.

'After Perran was born was a hard time. His mother died

bringing him into the world and he had to bring himself up more or less. Village raised him you could say, and he was theirs as much as he was his father's. It was a hard time.'

Ethan stops talking then and stares out across the water for a while, and when he turns back, Timothy is still looking at him, waiting.

'Always been on boats, from when he was a crawling babe, stowed down with the oilskins when we went out. No way for a child to be brought up, but it kept him in sight see?'

Ethan looks to see if Timothy is listening to him and pauses a moment to roll another cigarette. He lights it, takes a deep pull on it and continues.

'Never let him out of sight. And where better for him than on a boat, where we could keep watch on him? There were some as said a boat was no place for a child, but if ever there was a boy born of the sea it was Perran. And when he wasn't on the water he always kept an eye out for the boats. Watched them leave, watched them come back. Wasn't long before we came to rely on him being there. Like he was a good luck charm. Each of the skippers would put a hand on the top of his head before they sailed or left the beach. It was natural he was given the job down there, hauling up the boats when they came in, dragging them down to the water when they launched. Paid him with a cut of the catch, treated him fair. He moved into that house you're in as soon as he could. Can't say I blamed him.'

*Ethan watches from the café where he sits with his sometimes crew, drinking as he watches the other skippers gather on the beach. He watches as one of them laughs at something Perran says and then runs his hand roughly over Perran's tangled hair as he passes him and they both laugh again, and Ethan feels a thin lance of pain in his chest. Perran who understands the sea as if he was born to it. Perran who guides the boats in and out, who comes and goes as he pleases. Perran who lives alone and not in his father's house, who has joined this adult world before he should have, as though the rules don't apply to him.*

Ethan looks up and sees Timothy is still watching him, his gaze steadier than the rest of his body, which still jars and jolts with each wave that comes up against the boat. Waiting for more. There's challenge in Timothy's eyes for him to finish the story, and though he raises a hand to indicate to the other man he is done for now, Timothy stands his ground.

'There was a storm, see, and Perran was out on the rocks when he fell in, so they reckoned. Couldn't swim any better than the rest of us can, and that night it was fierce out. He washed up half a mile from the village, and a crew saw him on their way back in. We boarded his house up after that. You'll understand if some of us weren't crazy about it when you moved in.'

Ethan breaks Timothy's gaze, and moves forward suddenly, pushing past him to get to the lines for the nets they have cast. He feels anger rise up within him. He feels that Timothy is rubbing at a delicate fabric beneath his fingers and that whatever lies beneath this thin lining is starting to show through, as though the threads are starting to work themselves loose. As he starts to pull the nets in, he can feel, in their lightness, that he is pulling up nothing from the water.

# 12

# Timothy

TIMOTHY FEELS UNSURE what it is he has done to deserve this unasked-for gift. Whether it was joining Ethan on his boat when he could find no other crew, or encouraging him to strike out beyond the boundaries of the fleet. He wonders whether Ethan feels he is somehow responsible for the catch they made out there, that in some way his involvement that has brought new hunger to the fishermen, though he knows he played no part in it.

The only thing he knows for sure is Ethan now considers the matter closed. He has explained Perran. But Timothy's question remains, like a scar, or an itch that refuses to calm itself, an itch that has not accepted it has been scratched. Timothy cannot shake the feeling he is being lied to, and that Ethan's exposition conceals within it a veiled threat.

The wind is up now. It has come on quicker than Timothy thought possible, and spray from the tips of waves he cannot see blows in over the sides of the boat. There is no more fishing to be done, and the *Great Hope*'s hold is as empty as when they had left. Ethan has returned to the wheelhouse now and Timothy feels the cough of the engine through the soles of his feet as they turn back towards the shore, into the oncoming waves. He is unprepared for the first as it breaks over the bow and is glad he is holding the guard rail such is the shock of the cold and the force with which the water hits him. He wonders momentarily whether Ethan is pushing them on into the waves in the hope one will wash him overboard as it breaks over the deck. He pushes the thought from his head and concentrates instead on anticipating the next wave. The boat heaves from one peak to the next now, lurching forward and unable to find a rhythm, and waves break over the boat with no warning or sign of their approach. Timothy feels sickness rise up from his feet and radiate in towards his core from hands that are now starting to freeze. He looks back towards the wheelhouse hoping Ethan will swing the boat up out of this rough furrow so he can move back without fear of going overboard, but Ethan is busy pushing them on towards the shore, or is ignoring Timothy's plight on the deck. He looks out of the boat to the sea all around and tries to catch sight of the others, but the dancing lights have all disappeared now, and he wonders whether the other crews turned back before the sea had worked itself up like this.

Timothy edges himself backwards, his hand still gripping the guard rail, avoiding being drenched by the waves breaking over the sides. A crate that has worked its way loose from where it was secured slides across the deck and back. He is aware that this is not a storm, but just what the fishermen would call heavy weather.

Eventually, he manages to pull himself round into the shelter of the wheelhouse and sits himself down on a crate. There is barely room for two in the cabin and he is not sure he wants to be with Ethan in any case – Ethan, whose mood changes as quickly and erratically as the sea. He will sit out the weather on deck, in the lee of the wheelhouse. The journey back to shore drags and Timothy shivers as water soaks up beneath his coat and into the sleeves of his jumper. He tries to concentrate on keeping an eye out for the other boats, but there is still no sign of them, and the violent rocking of the boat overcomes him and he vomits, his head between his knees, onto the deck, over and again.

# 13

# Ethan

A S THEY RETURN towards the cove, Ethan jams the wheel, comes out from the cabin and watches Timothy for a while. Timothy is in a deep and uncomfortable sleep, wedged against a coil of rope on the thin walkway between the foredeck and the cabin. He shows no sign of waking, though Ethan checks a few times the closer they get to shore, and even as the *Great Hope* is dragged up the beach on the winch Timothy does not stir. Before he jumps down from the boat, Ethan lays an oilskin over the sleeping man. Then he makes his way up through the village towards Perran's. He is aware he might be seen, though the chances of it getting back to the incomer are slim.

At the side of the house, he tries the door and it opens. He is surprised, and stands for a moment with the handle held gently, before pushing through into the house. He has reached this point before and turned back so many times over the past ten years.

Inside, he has to check himself that this is the same house he knows, though he has only been inside once before, and under different circumstances. The shapes of the house – its walls, joints, lintels – are familiar, but inside looks different in the light and everything else is a reimagining, like a portrait in which the artist has seen his subject only at a distance and in poor light. It is an unfinished canvas and in places he sees the blank workings of the structure showing through. It feels raw and uncomfortable, but a different raw from the one he felt before. He is struck by the thought that the Perran he knew is being erased.

*Ethan watches from behind the curtain in the front room as the procession of villagers winds its way up past the house towards the service that is to take place on the hilltop above. There is no priest now, but those who knew him best will talk of Perran, of who he was and what he meant to them. There are some who will understand Ethan not being there, others will not. They will talk not only of Perran's absence, but of his too. Ethan can think of nothing he could say to the crowd gathered around the beacon and when the last of the procession has passed the house, he waits a while to see whether anyone else is following behind before turning his back to the window. As he waits for his breathing to calm, he tries to make out details in the darkness. Someone has been in and closed all the curtains and at the door of the living room his hand hovers over the light switch, but he lets it drop back to his side. He works his way slowly through the house, room by room in the darkness, learning the shapes and feel of the place. He treads carefully, slowly, so as not to disturb the furniture, though there is little enough of it to avoid, just a few darker shapes against the darkness. The stairs are steep and uneven, and as he makes his way up, he feels he is going to fall backwards.*

*Upstairs, he moves from room to room off the small landing until he finds the one that had been Perran's. It is at the front of the house, with a window overlooking the village, and beyond it the sea. Ethan stands for a while in the doorway, and sees, by what light enters through a gap in the curtains, a bed and by it a small table with a few items, indistinct in the darkness, a chest and little else. He looks around, to fulfil the purpose for which he came here, looking for some memento to take, a token that will allow him not to forget the events that brought him to this moment. There is nothing obvious. There are no small trinkets lying around, no personal belongings sitting on chests or tables, as though the house is resisting Ethan's attempts. He considers moving something, just to mark his time there, but finds he is unable to bring himself into contact with any of Perran's belongings, or anything that was connected to him. Instead, he sits on the bed for a while and feels the metal cold against his legs where they come into contact with the frame. He sits as waves of panic rise and crash over him, and stays hidden in the darkness of Perran's room for as long as he can stand it. When the feeling threatens to overwhelm him, he stands from the bed and walks quickly back through the house, crashing down the steep stairs, and out through the kitchen door. By the time he reaches the garden his breath comes in ragged coughs and he stands and breathes in the cold air and looks out through the branches and leaves that are left on the trees, to the cove below and the sea which he knows is there but can no longer see.*

He leaves, retracing his steps, as though Timothy might be able to sense he was there if he strays from the path he had trodden on the way in, and part of him wants to close his eyes as he does so and superimpose onto the house the Perran he knew. Part of him wants to close his eyes and to see nothing. As he walks down back through the garden, he sees, beneath the tall tree, a patch of earth newly turned over, neat and sad, and feels he has come across something that ought not to be disturbed.

Walking down the hill into the village, he watches seagulls tacking silently into the wind, broad wings outstretched, sometimes gaining ground, sometimes being pushed back and circling round to try again.

# 14

# Timothy

WHEN TIMOTHY COMES to, the first thing he is aware of is the stillness of the boat, and it takes him a while in the darkness to work out they are back on the beach and Ethan has gone. The boat and the beach around him are quiet. Timothy's clothes are soaked through and sit heavy and cold against his skin, and he stays where he is until he feels strong enough to pull himself up. He pushes aside the heavy oilskin and steadies himself against the wall of the wheelhouse, shivering, before limping up the hill towards Perran's.

Inside, he sheds his wet clothes and wraps himself in a blanket. He tries for a while to light the fire, but when the balls of paper and thin bones of wood he has put into the grate eventually take, the wind driving down the chimney pushes the smoke back into the room. As a grey cloud starts to fill the room he stamps through to the kitchen, fills a glass from the tap, and throws water over the small fire before retreating upstairs and dressing himself in several layers of clothes.

Throughout the night he remains cold, but eventually he returns to sleep and to a dream that he is standing by the water's edge. The sea is still and reflects the sky above – a perfect mirror image – and Timothy has the feeling he could walk forward onto the water, as though he might be stepping not into something liquid, but onto a solid veneer that only has the semblance of water. He feels something compelling him forward and he steps out and is only partly surprised to find the water does not rise up over his shoes, but remains beneath his feet. Even so, he edges forward carefully, moving slowly away from the shore. He has to force himself to stare ahead and to continue moving and it takes him some time moving in this way to come level with the mouth of the cove. At this point he looks back towards the village across the water and wonders why he had not noticed this phenomenon before, and why the villagers milling around on the beach or those who are walking up on the coast road do not seem to have noticed either, and show no interest in him as he walks out to sea. He continues to walk away from the village in the direction of the ships on the horizon. Behind him, he is aware he is leaving footprints that fade only moments after he has passed, as though he is creating in his path a short wake. He looks down to his feet to see the footprints as they are being created and immediately wishes he had not. Wanting only to look down to his feet, he cannot help but look beyond and below them to the vast depths beneath him, the space between his body and the seabed, hundreds of yards below. Timothy is suddenly aware of the surface he is walking on. Now he has seen the void beneath his feet he cannot unsee it, and he turns and starts to run back towards the shore, though even before he looks, he knows it will no longer be there. The land has dropped away and the only things that mark the difference between the surface upon which he is running and the sky are the container ships, that now form a complete, though expansive, circle around him. He picks one of the ships as a focus and runs towards it. He is not sure how long he runs, but at some point he is aware of another presence in the empty landscape. It is a house, sitting alone in the vast expanse, and he runs towards it. The house resembles Perran's house, though it is Perran's house as a child would render it. White walls and a tiled roof.

A door, flanked by a window on each side. He realises he is still running and has to slow as the house becomes suddenly much closer. When he enters, he sees the interior of the house consists of only one small room. Inside, there is a kitchen table covered with a cloth, and a chair at which he sits as he surveys the rest of the room. Against one of the walls is a cabinet along the shelves of which thin china plates lean. Beneath one of the windows is a porcelain sink and he stands to look at it more closely. The delicacy of the sink terrifies him, and as he looks around he notices the walls too are thin – terribly thin. He knows, beyond doubt, he could push a finger or a hand through any of the surfaces in the house without any difficulty, that he could tear the walls as he could tissue paper, to see what lies beneath. To avoid the temptation he pushes his hands deep into his pockets. He looks to the windows, and though he knows it was light when he entered the small house, he sees it is now dark outside, and the darkness is all but total. The room in which he sits radiates light, though he can see no source for this light, and it spills out of the windows to form a pool of brightness around the house. The ground around the house, he sees, is dark and contaminated and he can just make out through the windows steep walls rising up around him, walls that could be those of a quarry or of an immense scrapyard. He knows, without looking any further, that these walls rise to great heights around the house and he knows too they are what block out all the light from the sky above. The bright light emanating from the house flickers and falters and Timothy hears a roaring noise, as of a huge band of pressure approaching. He looks up and out of the window again and he sees that what he had identified as steep walls around the house are actually made of water, an impossibly tall, dark wave. The water seethes and he can see within it the detritus it has ripped up from the ground on its long journey to the small house, and buried far within the wave he

85

can make out some of the forms of the village and the coastline around, contained now within the crushing weight of thousands of tons of water. He sees, within the wave, the long bows of the container ships, weightless in the wave's body, and, though he cannot make them out clearly, he is sure he sees, suspended within its structure, the shapes of arms, legs and torsos too. As the wave approaches at what feels like impossible speed he feels the water draw all the heat from within the house, and the cold that penetrates far within him feels final and complete. Yet despite its speed, the water seems at the same time frozen, or slowed down, and the time it takes to reach the house is an age in and of itself, and he knows he must wait, looking out at the wall of water until it reaches and engulfs the small house. He wakes breathless and sweating in the cold of the bedroom and when he tries to move, he finds he is too weak to rise from the bed.

He lies like this for the next two days and nights, sweating and shivering. Unable to find any comfort in the bed, his sleep and dreams converge with his waking. Sometimes, in moments of drifting between the two states, he hears voices around his bed. Some of the voices are patient and concerned and others are angry and rave wildly at him, and others still are indistinct and he cannot work out from them what emotion the speakers are expressing. For the most part though, the voices sound to him like those of bureaucrats and he feels they are trying to impart to him information he is unable to absorb. He cannot make out from any of the speakers any words, just the sentiment of the words, just the impression they are important and that he should be paying attention. At one point he wakes, or dreams, he is not sure, to hear an argument taking place around him, an argument in which he feels he is the centre. And as his fever rages, he tries to follow the shadows of the speakers around the room, and the harder he listens to make sense of the voices, the further ahead of him they slip. Later, after it has been quiet again for some time, he hears the voice of one person talking to him and it is a voice that is familiar to him, though he cannot grasp to whom it belongs, and, over the deafening sound of his own breathing, he hears the words of the question that has been in his head for some time now. On waking one time in the pitch dark, he feels a more solid presence in the room, a figure sitting at the foot of the bed watching him. He knows it is Ethan and he tries to get some words out, but his throat is too parched by now, and no words escape. The effort of trying to talk pushes him back into sleep, and when he wakes again there is no one in the darkened room and he is unsure whether the glass of water sitting on the bedside table has been placed there while he slept, or whether it has been there the whole time.

When the fever breaks, the question is ringing loud in his head, too loud for him to ignore now, as though it had risen to make itself heard over the dull roar of the argument that raged around him during the worst of his sickness.

When he gets up he is still weak and he pulls a blanket around himself and stumbles downstairs into the kitchen. Standing on the linoleum floor, he lifts a large cardboard box from one of the kitchen surfaces and places it on the kitchen table. He runs a hand over the packets and tins looking for anything he has that is still edible. Among the disarray there is a half-full bottle of gin that came with him when he arrived. He pulls it out of the box and sets it down on the table in front of him, and when he has surveyed the rest of the box, he pours himself a glass.

The first taste of the gin makes him gag. He does not know how long it has been since he last ate, but the liquid burning its way down his throat takes his mind off the question in his head for a moment, and he drinks down the rest of the glass and pours himself another. Some time later, he has the urge to be in the company of others after being so long without conversation and he pulls on some clothes and walks down through the village.

# 15

# *Timothy*

'WHO WAS PERRAN?'

It is Timothy's opening question and he slurs it as Tomas approaches the bar. It is the first thing he's said all evening other than a few words he exchanged with the barman when he entered.

He has been there over an hour, working his way slowly through a beer, when the skippers of the fleet arrive. They acknowledge him, and the barman too, nodding towards them as they head towards a table as far away from the bar as it is possible to be in the small pub. By the time Tomas approaches the bar, the request has been waiting to be said for too long, and it comes out blunt and unlovely.

For a while it seems as though Tomas is going to wait for the barman to pour the pints and return to the others without answering him, but after the drinks are all gathered, he leaves the tray untouched in front of him and rests both hands on the edge of the bar. He then sits on one of the high bar stools and leans slightly towards the drinks, as though he is addressing them and not Timothy.

'You'll not hear about Perran from anyone here,' Tomas says quietly and turns again to go, and Timothy is considering begging him for more information when the other man turns back towards him.

'We held a eulogy for him at that table over there when

he didn't come back in, but you'll not hear a word of it from anyone here,' Tomas says, though he says it kindly. 'Nor any of the words that were read out for him up on the beacon after. Nothing I can tell you, nothing any of us can tell you.'

'And what about Ethan?' Timothy asks. 'He took it hard.'

'Ethan blames himself. Figures he was the part of the reason Perran went out onto the rocks that night. Happened not long after they started to draw closer together again, like things were about to change for the better then. Figured he was the jinx that sent Perran down. Though whether he still believes that, or that he could have said anything else that would have kept him off the rocks that night, I'm not asking him, and I suggest you don't bother him about it either.'

Tomas looks down at the tray for a moment.

'Afterwards, Ethan wouldn't believe he had gone, not for a long time. Kept a watch on Perran's place these ten years gone. I guess he'll have to give that up now.'

He continues to talk, but Timothy is no longer listening. He has the feeling he is no longer on land and that the village itself is a sea. He feels he has found himself surrounded by boats with their nets already cast into the water, spiralling in towards him in ever decreasing circles, and he knows he must retreat to Perran's house. He steps down from the barstool onto a shifting floor and his knees buckle beneath him. Arms flailing and the sensation of being caught and released. Asking the question over and over again. Pushes and shoves and raised voices, the voices muddled and indistinct. Glass shattering on the stone floor and he is caught and held. Being carried, by two, maybe three. Arguing and flailing. Cold air on his face. Sweating and cold. Silence. Sleep.

When Timothy wakes, it is to a dark room and, trying to reach his hand up to his face, he realises he cannot move and panics. He arches his body and kicks his legs, but whatever is restraining him holds fast and the effort causes him to cough. And while he coughs, what he can see of the room spins around him. After a minute or so, his eyes start to make out details. He is back in the bedroom at Perran's, lying in the narrow bed. Memories of being carried out of the bar come back to him, vague memories of being carried up through the winding streets to the house, along with the feeling someone is lying to him, or withholding the truth, and the question repeats itself over and over, though whether it remains unspoken inside him or he is repeating it out loud he is not sure. He has been laid on the bed and the sheets pulled tight over him, with bolsters of clothes laid out on either side of his body, presumably to stop him falling out of bed. He watches the walls rotate around him from where he lies and is aware he is not yet recovered from his sickness.

# 16

# Timothy

W HEN TIMOTHY IS well enough to pull himself out of the narrow bed again, late the next day, he sees his clothes are now folded and laid out on a chair, and wonders who has done this for him. He pulls a sheet around himself and walks slowly down through the house, trying to get his bearings again, though the house feels strange, transfigured yet again in his absence from it, and he is still unable to feel Perran in it. Feeling cold, he fills a bath and lies in it watching the steam rise from the water towards the unfamiliar ceiling until the water cools.

*The house has not been cleared*, the agent had said to him from behind a wide empty expanse of desk, and the words come back to him as he lies back in the bath. Timothy gets out of the bath quickly and wraps a towel around himself, and not bothering to dry off, he goes down to the kitchen. With a growing puddle of water gathering around his feet, he stands in front of the kitchen units and takes the handles of the cupboards nearest to him in both hands, opening both units simultaneously. There is the briefest moment in which he feels the open cupboards retain their darkness for a fraction longer than they should before they allow the light in. Both cupboards are empty, and so too are the drawers in the kitchen and the small pantry cupboard by the fridge. All he finds is yellowed newspaper lining the bottoms of all the drawers and shelves. He takes some of the paper out of one of the drawers and, on the paper that is still legible and that does not disintegrate as he pulls it up, he sees the articles are written in a language he does not recognise and the pictures that accompany the articles are blurred, as though the hand that took the photographs was shaking at the time they were taken. Going through all the rooms he finds the small items of furniture that have been there all along and the items he has brought to the house himself, but no sign of any clothes that were there before he arrived, no personal belongings. His search becomes more and more frantic but he finds nothing that could give him any clue about the previous owner, as though all evidence of who he was has been erased.

When Timothy has been all through the house, he dresses quickly and walks out through the kitchen door and around the side of the house to the smaller garden at the back. He searches the garden, turning over stones and moving his hands through the long grass where he thinks he sees objects below the grass line, but comes up with nothing. He walks round to the front and stands for a while by the tree beneath which he had buried the fish, and looks down the garden. At the bottom of the garden, the strips of paper caught on the thorns in the bare hedge hang like the markers of a roadside shrine, limp without the breeze and colourless in the fading light of evening.

He looks back towards the house, which is now a dark shadow against a darkening sky, and tries to picture Perran, but there is nothing of him to grasp, nothing to reveal him or suggest him to Timothy.

Perran is a shifting sand.

Timothy looks up at the upstairs windows and tries to imagine his wife, his children perhaps there too, looking back at him through those windows on a summer morning at some point a few years from now. His wife shouting down at him, asking would he like her to bring him tea in the garden. But he cannot transplant her face onto the scene, nor bring to mind now what the house itself looks like in the light.

How long he stands like this he does not know, but eventually the chill of the evening drives him indoors, where he sees, even by the bare bulb in the kitchen, the scale of the work there is still do.

Timothy realises he is hungry, and finds he cannot remember the last time he ate any proper food. Perhaps it was before he last went out on the water with Ethan, and he is not sure how many days and nights have passed since then. He picks up the empty bottle of gin from the table and throws it into the bin and investigates the fridge. He assembles what food has not already started to rot, turns the kitchen light off, and sits at the table to eat in the dark. Once he has eaten, he stacks the dirty plate with the others he has piled up by the sink and makes his way back up towards the bedroom. Though the darkness is almost complete, he does not turn on any more lights, wanting to avoid having to confront the unfamiliarity of this place. He feels his way across the bedroom, shuffling his bare feet forward to avoid colliding with anything in the room, and climbs into bed, and when he closes his eyes the feeling of unfamiliarity follows him into his own head and he lies still and waits for sleep to come, though it is a long time in coming. He lies still and listens to the sounds in the house and wonders what more he will find changed in the morning, what more will be unfamiliar to him.

When morning comes, he still feels weak, but Timothy feels the need to move, to rid himself of the cold that had seeped into his bones somewhere out on the water and that he has been unable to shake for however many days his illness has taken up. He pulls on his running clothes and, jogging and walking alternately for a few yards at a time, makes his way out slowly along the coast road, and the feeling that has grown in him overnight starts to shift and fade. It takes him a long time to warm himself through and he is way beyond the village by the time he is warm enough to stop and wait for his breathing and his heart to slow. When he stops, he looks down from the road at the waves breaking over the rocks and remembers Ethan's warning. He wonders whether the illness through which he has now passed was related to his earlier swim, some prolonged incubation period of a waterborne virus, or brought on purely by the effects of exposure to the cold and the waves. At this point, a mile or so after the houses have thinned out, the landscape becomes more and more featureless. To one side of the road the water and the rocks and the white foam that separates the rocks from the sea, to the other side fields, surrounded by walls made up of tightly packed stones, and the further he runs, the less he finds he is able to judge time and distance in this landscape that repeats itself over and again.

There is a thin mist on the ground in the fields beyond the low wall that separates them from the road, and through it the uneven ground looks like it too could be water from the way it dips, rolls and peaks. For a moment the road feels more like a narrow bridge across an expanse of sea, a long ribbon connecting an island to the mainland.

Some of the fields contain, within them, large clumps of trees or large stones around which the farmers must navigate their tractors to plough or harvest the field. At least a couple of the fields are host to stone structures and, from where he stands now, Timothy sees the one in the field closest contains an opening into the earth. As he looks closer he can make out the arch of a door, with a lintel stone above the entrance. He turns towards it, climbs the wall, and lowers himself carefully over into the field. He jogs over to the structure and stands looking down into the opening between the stones. The lintel stone casts a shadow, even in the half-light of early morning and what light there is does not reach far down through the opening.

There is a steep step down from the field level into the cave and he can see nothing beyond the patch of earth directly beneath the lintel stone, worn smooth and grassless. He steps towards the doorway in order to see further in and stands just shy of the shadow it casts. Unable to see further, he lowers himself down into the darkness to see better what lies beyond. He feels the cold rising up from the ground as he descends and it brings to mind a memory of lowering himself into the burning cold of the sea. The floor is deeper than it had looked originally and when his feet touch the floor he is in the shadow, unable to see anything in front of him. He edges forward, waiting for his eyes to accustom themselves to the darkness. There is a rustling in front of him and two heavy bodies hurtle out of the darkness and Timothy is knocked back sharply onto the smooth floor. Thin feet jab at his head and he raises his hands to protect his face, gripped by a panic that threatens to overwhelm him and he flails his legs and keeps his hands and arms up over his face and ears as the assault continues. A heavy body lands on him and he struggles to breathe beneath its smothering weight, and the scrabbling resumes. He feels something sharp connect with his mouth and there is a sudden pressure on his chest and then there is silence. He tries to bring his breathing under control and tries to fight the feeling he needs to run from this place and forces himself to lie still. Lying on his back in the darkness, he feels the weakness his fever has left him with start to spread through his body.

When he stands and emerges into the light, he looks around and as his eyes adjust again, he sees two sheep, huddled together, just a few yards away in the field, eating grass with some urgency and ignoring him and he is glad he has not been seen by anyone else, panicking over a couple of sheep trapped in a cave in a country field. Unnerved, he jogs back to the field boundary, climbs the wall again and turns to run back towards the village.

He slows to a walk a hundred feet or so from the house, and looks at it alongside the others on the row. As he does, he has the feeling if it were not for its position on the road, flanked as it is by two other houses in the same style, he could walk past Perran's and not know it at all.

Back inside and sitting at the kitchen table, Timothy scribbles an advert for a decorator onto a piece of card he has ripped from one of the packing boxes, which he later takes down to the café by the beach. It seems to be the only place open aside from the pub and the store, and the girl behind the counter says he can put it on the wall by the door for a week.

After only a few hours a note is pushed through the door of his house. He reads it, puts it on the kitchen table and watches it for a while, before consigning it to the kitchen bin. It was another bad idea.

The next time he walks down to the seafront, and passes the café, the same waitress who told him he could put up his advert catches him as he walks by the open door.

'You want someone to help with that house?'

He nods, though he is not now sure that he does.

'Tracey. My sister. She'll do it fine. She's done work in most people's houses round here. She'll do fine. I'll send her over 'round three.'

And it is arranged. The waitress has retreated back into the café. Though he does not want anyone to come to the house now, he cannot find a good enough reason to put her off, so he continues his walk between the café and the winch house propped up against the wall that separates the road from the beach.

Clem is sitting outside on the deep concrete step looking out at the sea and Timothy sits down next to him. Clem says nothing, and Timothy wonders whether he has heard him arrive.

'I ran out beyond the village this morning,' Timothy says. 'I had a look at those stone structures, the ones in the field. Do you know what they are, what they were? They look old. Are they storehouses? Or graves? Are they symbolic of something?'

'The barrows?' Clem replies and his voice is far away. 'No, no one knows what they're there for. No meaning in them I know of.'

Clem settles back into his silence and after a minute or so Timothy wonders whether the other man has forgotten he is there.

'Tell me about Perran then,' Timothy says. 'Or at least tell me why you won't talk about him.'

The winchman says nothing, but continues to stare out to where the gulls sit on the rocks at the mouth of the cove, waiting on the return of the fleet. Timothy has a feeling it is not Clem sitting next to him at all, but that he is out with the birds on the rocks, watching with them in hope of a catch for the fleet, and in hope of their safe return. That the man beside him is a golem, an empty shell left to sit by the water while its inhabitant walks elsewhere. Timothy stands and walks down off the concrete step onto the stones, and Clem speaks before he has gone five yards.

'What is there to tell?'

Clem's voice still sounds as though he is talking at a distance.

'What is there I could tell you would make him real to you?'

He is silent then a while longer and Timothy thinks he is finished and the stones crunch beneath his feet as he turns to walk on.

'You want to hear me tell you he was a good man, and one who worked hard for his lot. A grafter. You'll want to hear he was the best of us, the one who looked out for all the rest and never tired, and never bitched and never moaned when the fish dried up, and kept the fleet going until they made their way back.'

Timothy feels each of the words as though they are stones

from the beach pitched into dead calm water. Each one drops into the deep and makes its way down through forests of kelp to settle heavy on the sea floor. Timothy feels his legs start to buckle beneath him and he wants to sit down again before he falls down onto the stones.

'You want me to tell you he was gifted. Or a gift. A talisman. That when I took over from him, I was stepping into shoes I could not hope to fill. There's some will tell you that, sure.'

More stones falling one after the other into the water, each one small and heavy, and each one heavier than the last. The words reach him as if transmitted over a vast distance and he feels each fall on him like a mote of infinite density that punctures and passes through him.

'What do you want him to be? What do you want to feel about him? You want to feel proud? You want to feel he was okay, that he lived out a life he was happy with?'

The distance with which Clem had spoken earlier is receding now, and with each sentence, he gets louder and closer to Timothy, though as far as he can tell, the older man has not moved from where he is sitting, on the concrete step. Clem's voice has risen too, as though the question has dragged him back from his place out with the birds on the rocks, and his words are sharp round the edges, as with smooth stones that break and splinter when they are thrown down among others on the beach. Timothy wants to be far away from Clem now. He wants to be far away from this village, out in the open space of the sea, though as he looks out that way, the line of container ships on the horizon stares backs at him. He stands and walks away from Clem, who is still sitting outside the hut, staring out onto the water, and the winchman's words follow him until he is out of sight of the beach and back up on the road.

Timothy wanders back up through the village and as he

walks along the top row, he sees there is a girl or woman waiting for him on the front step of the house.

Tracey's bleached hair makes her look younger than she is, and when she moves it aside from where it has fallen across her face, he sees her skin, sun-scarred and pocked. Standing on the doorstep talking to him, she is already looking around him into the hallway with open curiosity, though why this is he cannot understand, as she has arrived to work in the house and she will be inside soon enough. He wonders again whether this move has been a mistake, though she is here now and soon enough in the house, wandering from room to room, looking appraisingly, a little shocked, unimpressed, he cannot tell. He leaves her to her exploration and sits in the kitchen, not wanting to put the kettle on in case she takes it as an invitation to stay any longer.

'I know what this house needs,' she says. 'Leave it to me, I'll make a start now.'

There is something suggestive in the tone of her voice. Timothy considers telling her he has not made up his mind yet about taking her on for the job, but she has taken out a notepad already and is scribbling in it with a pencil stump. He feels obliged to take her instruction, and he picks up his jacket from the back of a kitchen chair and leaves through the side door.

By the time Timothy returns to the house, Tracey has gone, though as he walks through the house to check, he has the passing thought she might be waiting for him in the bedroom. She is not, but she has left behind her the smell of smoke, which lingers throughout the rooms and on the stairs, and he finds a small pile of cigarette ends by the doorstep. He walks through the house and sees she has been trialling swatches of paint over the walls in the front room, lines of powder blue by the chimneybreast. It's not what he would have chosen, and he starts to wonder, now he has invited someone else into the house to make decisions, what his role here might be. He paces the house and thinks on the different ways in which he might rid himself of her.

He decides the next time he sees Tracey, he will tell her it is all a terrible mistake, and that he will pay her for the work she has done so far but that she need not come back again. He pats the pocket where earlier he put the spare key for her to use, and he is glad he forgot to pass it over to her.

That night, as he lies in bed waiting for sleep to come, he hears noises around the outside of the house, and several times he gets up and looks out of the windows down into the garden. When he looks though, the darkness is too thick to make anything out, and whether the sounds are of animals or people he cannot tell. He reminds himself he bolted the doors before he came upstairs and, though he listens hard now, he hears nothing more and eventually he falls asleep. When he wakes it is still dark and the sense of unease remains with him and he lies staring up at the ceiling that he still does not recognise as belonging to this place.

After that he sleeps and wakes and the lines between the two states blur until it starts to become light. He opens the curtains and watches from his bed as the sun comes up over the sea. Not a postcard sunrise, but a gradual lightening of the black into greys, and the greys into blues, and later, greens.

When he goes downstairs and opens the curtains in the front room he is surprised to see, on the small strip of concrete which circles the house, separating it from the garden, a man. He is standing with his back to the house, facing out towards the sea. He wonders how long Ethan has been standing there, and Ethan, as though he senses him at the window, turns to face Timothy.

'You coming then?' Ethan says through the window and Timothy looks around at all he must still do, at the bare floors, at the flecks of wallpaper still clinging to the stripped walls, at the fireplace he has stopped stocking with wood despite the cold.

'I've got a lot . . .' Timothy lets the words trail off as he sees Ethan's expression.

'You're coming then,' Ethan says.

Timothy nods and retreats upstairs to get dressed into warmer clothes.

Ethan's is the last of the boats left on the beach. Once they have climbed aboard they settle into silence, and Timothy sits on the gunwales as Ethan prepares the boat. Clem, sitting in the tractor, is impatient for them to launch. He does not acknowledge either man, and when he has dragged the boat down to the water, he unhooks it without a word, and heads back up the beach.

It is a calm morning, and the lack of clarity in the horizon does not resolve itself in the weak sunlight. Timothy looks back up towards the house and hopes Tracey will return and take the hint from the locked doors, or that she will have decided already to leave him be. The other boats in the small fleet are spread out as far as they can be within the boundaries of the container ships today, not bunched up as they are when the sea is rough.

They have been out maybe four hours, working at setting, shooting and pulling up the empty nets, before Ethan speaks, as though to reward Timothy for obeying his rules. Sensing Ethan standing close by, Timothy looks up from where he is kneeling on the deck, stands, and pushes his frozen hands into his coat pockets.

'Clem says you've been asking about Perran again.'

*Timothy and Lauren walk beneath autumn trees ablaze with colour. The trees are mostly beeches, acre upon acre of them run through with a criss-cross of paths for walkers and joggers. They follow a path that leads them past a series of sculptures carved* from fallen trees. The sculptures are mostly hidden, or obscured beneath the piles of leaves that have drifted around them. They walk slowly. Lauren is heavily pregnant and they stop at each bench they come to and watch leaves spiral down from the trees. The autumn sun still has some strength in it and it lights the wood in a way that makes it feel like the wood is creating its own light. Each leaf that falls seems illuminated as it passes through a thick band of light. Timothy and Lauren do not speak much as they walk, though occasionally she takes his hand, or he hers, just briefly as they walk along the path. Sometimes it is little more than the backs of their fingers that touch, like the leaves of two trees brushing against each other in the breeze – small reminders they are sharing this experience. Above the tree canopy, the wind is blowing, but though they can hear it overhead, all they feel of it are its effects, the leaves falling around them.

The path they follow eventually leads out and away from the woods and they stand for a while at the point where the trees are replaced by more open woodland, and where the path leads off between lower bushes and younger trees. Lauren turns back to return along the path into the woods again and Timothy follows.

As they walk back along the path, the sight of a young family beneath one of the trees causes Timothy and Lauren to stop a short way off and they watch as they play. The parents are sitting next to one another with their backs against a broad tree trunk, their hands joined and partially buried in the leaves that surround the tree. A child of three or four is running around the trunk in ever decreasing circles, dipping to the ground every few seconds to scoop up handfuls of leaves which she then throws into the air. The girl laughs loudly as the leaves cascade around her. As her circles tighten towards the tree trunk, she gathers up larger handfuls of leaves and saves them for the point at which she passes her parents, throwing them high into the air above them and racing around the tree as the leaves fall, blanketing *the young couple. Her parents join her laughter and Timothy and Lauren walk on back towards the car park. As they leave the scene, Timothy feels Lauren's fingers intertwine with his own and she squeezes his hand.*

# 17

# *Timothy*

TIMOTHY DOES NOT see the crowd on the beach until he feels the stones crunch under the boat's keel. The gathering is of a similar size to the one he saw when they brought in their catch, only this one waits silently in the dark, hanging back against the concrete beach wall. The *Great Hope* grounds and Clem comes forward with the winch cable. Both Timothy and Ethan are silent too, and Timothy wonders how much of this Ethan knows about, how much he was expecting, how much he has been involved in, and whether he is aware of what is to happen next.

The winch cable takes the strain and the boat judders forward up onto the stones. There is no one guiding the boat and it tips over to one side, and both Timothy and Ethan hold onto the gunwale, to avoid being pitched over the side. Once the boat clears the waterline, the machinery halts, and the crowd, until now held in shadow by the lights from the houses on shore, starts to push forward. Other than the stones underfoot and a soft murmuring where the sea laps at the shore behind them, there is no other sound.

Timothy thinks he recognises the outlines of some of the other fishermen among the crowd of twenty or so. Clem has joined them again now, and as Timothy looks over the edge, he walks forward a couple of steps, a boat hook on a pole in his hand.

'We'd like you to come down.'

He says it softly, as though he is talking to an animal that needs to be reassured, placated, to a dog that may bite. As though it is Timothy who is the threat rather than the threatened. When Timothy makes no move, Clem taps the side of the boat with the pole gently.

Timothy looks behind him to Ethan, and Ethan shrugs and nods his agreement to Clem's words.

Timothy releases his grip on the boat and stumbles down to the rail that is closest to the beach. The crowd backs up a little to let him down, though Clem remains where he is, watching Timothy carefully, and when he finds his feet on the beach, Timothy is close enough to hear the other man's breath.

'What's this about then?' Timothy asks. 'A welcome home party for tired fishermen?'

'Just time to talk is all,' says Clem. His voice retains the same calm, quiet quality as before and he starts to walk up the beach, pausing only to let Timothy catch up with him. There is a moon behind the thin cover of clouds above and, as they walk through the gathering, Timothy can see a few faces he recognises – Rab, Tomas, Jory, Santo, Tracey, the girl from the café – though as he looks around none of them will meet his eye. Towards the back of the crowd, standing aside from the others, he sees another figure he recognises, that of the woman in grey, who is looking in on the scene, though it seems to Timothy that she is an observer and not part of the mob.

The crowd parts for Timothy and Clem. Timothy wonders whether the gathered men and women are all going to fall in behind them and follow, but they stay where they are, as the two men climb up off the beach.

They walk up through the village, and what light spills out from the houses illuminates Clem's face. He looks troubled. They walk up past Perran's and through a gap between two of the houses at the end of the row, and over a stile into a field. A rut around the edge of the field leads them further away from the houses and up onto the beacon and they slow down to pick their way up a path that is littered with loose stones. At one point, Timothy trips and pitches forward, but Clem is close enough to him to stop him falling. He waits while Timothy regains his balance and helps him find his feet again. When they reach the summit, by the stubby white marker stone, Clem comes to a stop and leans heavily on the boat hook, while he gets his breath back. Timothy turns towards Clem and is about to speak, and as he does so Clem swings round towards him and puts a hand square on Timothy's chest.

The wind is strong at the top of the hill and brings with it a dull roar of white noise, and when Clem talks he has to raise his voice as the wind blows around them and down through the village.

'We answered your questions as best we can, now it's time to leave them be,' he says and turns slightly so his face is now turned back towards the village. 'It won't do any good you asking them any more.'

Timothy shrugs and feels Clem's hand press harder against his chest.

'Perran's ours,' Clem says, and this time he moves closer in, and speaks low and soft into Timothy's ear. 'See?'

Clem is so close now he has blocked out the wind that whips around them and Timothy can now hear each breath the other man takes.

'You'll not know him. Not here and not ever,' says Clem, and without moving away he waves the boat hook out over all of the village below. 'You want me to tell you he stood up here and breathed in the air and looked out on this scene in the morning as the light came up, and as the sun rose over the sea. And at noon when it was hot and there was no shade and in the afternoon when he watched the boats out on the water and thought they were all he needed to see in the world, and later in the evening when the sun set and the sea was ablaze. You want me to tell you he's buried here, under the marker stone, or down there in the barrows, from where he could keep watch on us. You'll want me to talk until you know him. Am I wrong?'

Timothy can feel Clem's breath on the side of his face he is so close now.

'He's not,' Clem continues. 'Not buried here, nor down in the village, nor out at sea. You'll not find a headstone, though you might look for one as long as you please. So take your questions and leave them be. Take them away from here. Or, if you stay, stay and keep them to yourself.'

Clem's arms fall to his side and he takes a couple of steps back then, his job done.

'Tell me then,' says Timothy. He cannot help the question rising from some well inside and Clem turns on the spot and swings the boat hook towards him with a speed Timothy does not expect. It hits him square on the chest and knocks him to the ground. Clem is standing over him now, shaking with what Timothy can only assume is anger, with the boat hook raised, covering him so he cannot get back up. Timothy can taste blood in his mouth. After a moment that lasts an age, Clem's breathing shallows and he moves the boat hook away. As he backs away from Timothy, the moonlight catches his face again. By it, Timothy sees a man twisted in frustration or exasperation. It is not a face that wants to do him harm. There is something paternal in it perhaps and it occurs to Timothy that Clem believes he is doing him a favour.

Clem backs up a few more paces from Timothy, who is lying, still in shock, on the ground. He turns away and then back towards Timothy, and Timothy wonders whether he is going to return the finish the job. He still has the hook in his hand,

and he is raising and lowering it as though he is rehearsing a motion in his head that he is unaware is being played out by his body. But eventually he drops, or rather throws, the hook on the ground and walks away from Timothy.

'Why bring me up here to tell me this then?' Timothy shouts down after Clem as he walks away down the hillside. 'Why drag me up a hill to tell me what questions I can and can't ask?'

But Clem has given up on Timothy now and is walking away. He does not look back, but leaves Timothy on the ground in the dark of the hillside with the wind whipping around his ears, feeling as though he has been sucked out to sea by an unstoppable tide and stranded far away.

Timothy lies on his back and the cold from the wind and from the ground below seeps into his body through his clothes. The blood in his mouth tastes metallic and the question repeats itself as if it is on a loop, quiet and insistent and endless.

# 18

## *Timothy*

B Y THE TIME Timothy arrives back at the house, the wind has dropped and he finds the house in darkness, though from the road he can hear the sound of a door swinging against its frame in the wind. As it comes into view, he can see the front door is open, revealing a darkness darker than that of the night outside. He walks around the side of the house to the door he uses now and sees that too is open. He approaches slowly and when he gets to the doorway, he runs his fingers over the splintered wood where the lock has come away from the doorframe, and walks through into the kitchen. He tries the switches on the wall just inside the door, but the lights will not turn on, and nor will the lights in the hall or the sitting room when he comes to those. There is a sharp chemical smell in the air that thickens the deeper he walks into the house.

He feels the carpet wet underfoot and after cracking his shins on furniture that is lying strewn across the floor, he walks more carefully and stops each time he feels something in his way. A fallen chair, its legs in the air, a bookcase upended, the pages of novels and textbooks soaking up whatever liquid has been poured onto the carpets. He moves like this for several minutes, slowly investigating the house in the darkness. He heads upstairs to look for the torch he knows is in his bag under the bed, but by the time he has found the torch he realises he does not want to see the extent of the damage and he leaves it where it is. In the bedroom, he is aware the bed frame has been pulled out of alignment and there is a pile of his clothes tipped out of drawers onto the mattress, and some of the upstairs windows have been put through. The wind comes cold into the room and through onto the landing. Timothy closes the door of the bedroom, but makes it no further than the doorway to the sitting room, where he slumps against the doorframe and allows himself to slide down to the floor. With his head held in his hands and his knees up around his ears he begins to sob, uncontrollably for some time and then because he allows it to continue. Later, he finds the strength to stand again, though only to make his way across the darkened sitting room to the armchair in the corner of the room, which, he can see by its silhouette, is still standing. He checks it and finds it has escaped being doused in whatever liquid covers the floors. He sits down and, taking off only his shoes, tries to recline the chair, though the mechanism will not work, and he pulls a blanket over himself and tries to push himself as deep into the cushions as possible, to wait for the morning to arrive.

In the village below, the church bells start to ring, slow and persistent, and the sound makes its way into the house and continues late into the night.

He spends the night sleeping and not sleeping on the chair and at some point he dreams. He is standing, alone, by the side of the coast road, the glare of a full and heavy moon bearing down on the sea in front of him and on the fields behind. Both the sea and the fields are still and calm under the weight of the moonlight and the reflection of the moon on the water amplifies its glare. He is waiting for something he knows is about to happen, so when it does happen, it is not a surprise. A slight movement in the water, a susurration from the fields behind, and they emerge, like some great exodus or migration of animals, pulled out of the sea by the moon all at once.

They emerge in their hundreds, or perhaps in their thousands, pouring out of the sea and he cannot believe the sea is able to hold so many of them. They emerge in numbers too great for him to take in and, overwhelmed, he turns away from them, only to find they are emerging too from the barrows and are filling the fields. Perran upon Perran upon Perran. Timothy knows they are all Perran and that each one of them has within him the potential for infinite variety, though all the figures before him are faceless and featureless. At that moment he feels he knows for each of the Perrans emerging every decision each of them has made and will ever make, and still they pour forth from the sea and from the ground. They crowd towards him, not out of any knowledge of him or sense that he is there, but because they fill all the space around, and they continue to come until they block out the light from the moon, and the darkness takes him.

In the early morning, as morning light begins to make its mark on the darkness, he is able to see the full extent of the damage. The damp underfoot is the paint he had bought for the walls, poured out over the new carpets. There are tens of pairs of footprints walking through it in every direction and the paint shows the path the townsfolk took through the house and out into the garden. The curtains he had hung have been ripped from their hooks and lie on the floor, soaking up paint, and through the window he can see splintered items of furniture spread out across the grass in front of the house. He walks outside among the wreckage and beneath the large tree he finds a pile of disturbed earth and by it, in rows, the disintegrating bodies of the fish he buried a week previously. They are laid out next to one another on the ground, an array of rotting fish, pale and luminescent. Scattered around them is a halo of scales, and, as a slight breeze passes through the garden, they shift and float upwards and then back down to the ground. Timothy sits beside the fish and looks around him at the scene. After a while, he rouses himself and, after looking and not finding anything else suitable to use for the job, gets down onto his knees and uses his hands to re-excavate the hole. One by one, he replaces the fish with care in their grave and covers them over with soil.

He rises from the ground and goes back into the house where he walks from room to room again, picking up and then replacing on the floor the books he had brought with him, small and splintered pieces of furniture. It reminds him of images of the aftermath of a hurricane he once saw on the news. It feels elemental somehow, rather than something human, though the footprints throughout the house belie this thought.

He works his way through the upstairs and as he inspects the broken windows in the front bedroom he sees there is something different about the scene below, something unusual about the village in front of him. From where he is, he can see that the mouth of the cove looks like it belongs to another place altogether such is its transformation, as though it has been entirely rearranged overnight. Wanting to be anywhere but inside the house, he makes his way back downstairs and locates his spare waterproof on a hook behind the door in the kitchen. The coat has escaped the violence and he pulls it on over his clothes, and leaving the house behind him, he walks down through the village.

It is only when he comes out from between the narrow rows of houses fronting onto the beach that he sees the sea has risen overnight and the beach has been entirely drowned, though there has been no storm and no warning of high tides. The water has risen up above the height of the concrete wall that separates the beach from the village. The roof of the winch house is still visible, and sections of railing that run along the boundary between the beach and the road poke up out of the water. The café, too, is now an island floating in the sea. It looks as though it has been unhitched from the land and stays where it is only for lack of movement in the water or air. The coast road, too, is under water along the sea front, and the waves lap at the foot of the houses on the other side of the road. At either end of the submerged beach, the road rises out of the water, as though a section of it has been dipped into the dark water for treatment. As Timothy stands on the steps of one of the houses that face directly onto the sea and looks out on this newly created scene, he sees the lights of the fleet converging on the cove mouth from their night's fishing.

Timothy looks around to see if there is anyone else there to witness the flood. At first it appears he is alone, though he sees to his left, where the coast road emerges from the water, a blue car with dark-tinted windows is slowing to a halt just a few feet from the water. As he watches, the passenger door opens and a figure steps out of the car. It is the woman and, though she looks straight towards him, if she sees him she does not acknowledge it. She looks perturbed by what she sees and she stands for a while examining the scene. Timothy waits and watches for her to get back into the car and reverse up the hill on the narrow road, but she remains where she is, as though she is trying to unravel a complex problem.

He plays through in his mind a scenario in which each morning he wakes to find the sea has risen another few feet overnight and has claimed another portion of the village until it reaches Perran's house and the waves lap at the door.

For a while, the only observers of this scene are Timothy and the woman in grey, and when the villagers start to emerge from their houses, both of them retreat, she to behind the tinted glass of the car beside which she is standing, and he to Perran's.

When he arrives back at the house he tries to assess the damage there with a more objective eye. He walks again from room to room, righting pieces of furniture, working out which pieces he can salvage. In the living room, after lifting the large bookcase back against the wall, he picks up books from the sodden floor, their pages splayed out, as though they want to soak up as much as possible of the chaos that ran through the house the night before.

Timothy works on reclaiming the house for the rest of the day and sees no one. He assumes the rest of the village is preoccupied with the damage caused to the seafront. Working through the house, he starts to pile his newer furniture together on the patch of grass outside the front of the house that is still yellowed and flattened from the furniture he had removed from the house weeks earlier. When the pile reaches head height he fills some of the empty drawers and cupboards with newspaper and sets light to it. The chemical-soaked furniture takes quickly and burns with a dark acrid smoke that sticks to the back of Timothy's throat. He looks down towards the beach, but the attention of the village is still turned towards the high waters below and the fire and its fume-heavy smoke go unnoticed.

As Timothy watches the fire spread he feels a strong emotion rise up within him, surging to the surface, though even as it does he knows it is not because of the damage to the house, or the hostility of the village. As the fire builds, he feeds it with the books that are beyond repair. He stands as close to the flames as he can bear in order to dry the tears as they form and wonders what he has done to bring this down on himself.

# 19

# *Ethan*

THE FOLLOWING MORNING the village descends again to the beach to find the waters have fallen away as suddenly as they had risen. Ethan, when he emerges from his house, is drawn down to the seafront like all the others, and he finds the beach crowded by the time he gets there.

The water was calm as they had entered the cove the day before, and from the sea, the village had looked like a different place entirely. They had secured the boats to the railings that ran in a line, like a fence bisecting a field of snow; the only indication there was when they returned of the boundary between the beach and the road.

The state of the café on the front shows the violence of the water's retreat. Anne and two girls who help her out in the café stand huddled together outside the entrance amid the debris of tablecloths, salt cellars and menus that have been dragged out of the building by the retreating water. The door hangs uselessly, wrenched from its hinges. Further below scattered across the beach are the café's chairs and tables. The two girls look to be the only thing holding Anne up, and they are talking to her in low voices, words he cannot hear. The sound of their voices is comforting and, not wanting to interrupt them, he walks around them in a wide arc.

The winch house is still standing, though it is as though the sea has tried to suck out its contents through the door.

The machinery within has been uprooted and now blocks the doorway in a twisted confusion of metal. Ethan hears the sound of metal on metal from inside, and he looks in to see Clem has climbed in over the machinery blocking the door and is shifting things around in the darkness of the hut. As he gets closer, he sees that Clem is picking up whatever is loose and lying about on the floor and hurling it against the machinery, inflicting more damage on what is already damaged.

The waves on the shore are playing with empty crates and creels, pushing them up onto the stones and pulling them back again. The cove is littered with plastic bags, polystyrene blocks, floating on the oil-slick water, and they are slowly being sucked out through the mouth of the cove with the tide. Clem's tractor, too, has been dragged down from its place at the top of the beach and it now sits a few metres out into the cove. Only the steering wheel of the tractor and the back of the driver's seat are visible.

The *Great Hope* lies on the stones listing over to one side, as do the other boats that returned the day before. All the boats left on the beach have been dragged as far down the beach as the chains securing them to the railings will allow, and they strain on them like dogs against their leashes. All the loose ropes and chains attached to the dividing wall are also outstretched and are laid out in a series of parallel lines down the beach and on into the water. Ethan feels if he picked one of the lines up, he could pull the sea and the sky towards him.

It takes him a while to understand what is wrong with the scene, and at first he thinks he must be mistaken, but as his eyes follow the outstretched cables and ropes down towards the beach, he sees it is no longer the same beach, and the stones that make it up are no longer the same stones. It is as though while the space remains the same, it has been filled with items that are similar but not the same. He feels as though everything has been replaced by someone who knows this place well, but who has had to reconstruct it from memory. He looks around and the feeling compounds itself and although when he focuses on any one thing – the rocks at the mouth of the cove or the stones on the beach – and they match the image in his memory, he suddenly feels like a stranger in this place.

As he looks down on the beach he starts to feel panic welling up in him. And in between the outstretched ropes, pulling their way to the sea, he sees the first cracks. Thin black lines that run the length of the beach from where they emerge out of the water, up through the stones towards the concrete wall. The lines are barely perceptible and he wonders whether he is actually seeing them at all. He looks around to see if anyone else has noticed, but the villagers are going about their business and show no sign they have seen anything more unusual than the devastation left by the high tide.

He looks around for Timothy, as though Timothy might be the only person who might understand what he is experiencing, but Timothy is nowhere to be seen.

## 20

# *Timothy*

TIMOTHY GOES THROUGH the house laying down sheets over the bare floorboards and, using the remaining dustsheets, he covers what remains of the ruined furniture and the walls as best he can.

He sits on the narrow mattress and fills the canvas bag that has been lying beneath the bed since he arrived. The bag has escaped the damage and he shoves in all the clothes that are not beyond repair and takes it down to the car, though as he emerges from the house he notices the passenger window has been smashed, more damage he had not seen before. He fishes out a shirt from the canvas bag, wraps it round his hand and clears the broken glass from the window frame and from the seats as best he can, though even as he does, he can see pools of broken glass accumulating in the seat well and around the handbrake. The damage does not appear, at first glance, to extend beyond the broken window and when he has cleared most of the glass, he places the canvas bag on the passenger seat and gets in at the driver's door. He sits there for a while, looking back at the house with its door left swung wide open. There's no point closing it. His shoulders sag and, feeling an emotion start to pass over him, the first tentative waves that lap at the shore as the tide turns its force upon the land, he twists the key.

The engine coughs, tries to turn over and gives up. He tries again and this time it coughs again, but more weakly, and the third time he tries it gives no response. He is calm at first and then the frustration rises in him faster than he thinks possible and when he opens the door to get out, he pushes it outward with enough force for something in the hinges to give. He leans against the door and then pushes it again with his full weight behind it and feels the mechanism break completely and he leaves it hanging from its frame like a broken arm.

Timothy walks between the house and the car several times, pacing between the two open doors, unable to pick one. Eventually, he reaches in through the smashed window and picks the bag from the passenger seat of the car and takes it into the house again.

Back inside, he places the canvas bag back on the bed, returns downstairs, pulls one of the remaining chairs over to the window in the front room and spends the rest of the day staring out at the sea.

The next day he walks down into the village and places a card on the noticeboard outside the village store, which is far enough back from the seafront to have escaped the high waters and is still open for business. Then he walks back up to Perran's and takes up the same position by the window again.

# 21

# Timothy

T HERE IS A knock at the door and Timothy stirs in his chair but does not move. There is another knock.

'Heard you've got car trouble.'

The voice comes in through the kitchen, through the door he has not bothered to close. Timothy stands from the chair by the window and walks through to the back of the house where he finds Tomas, who is appraising the wreck of Timothy's car. Timothy stares, wondering whether Tomas has come to gloat, or to see how the damage to the house looks in the light of day. In the nights since the break-in he has pictured all four of the skippers at the front of the mob that stormed the house, tearing down pictures and furniture.

But Tomas does not look as though he is there to gloat. He looks concerned. At the state of the car, and at the state of Timothy, who has not washed or shaved for three days now and has barely eaten either. He is aware from Tomas's stare that he does not look like a well man.

'There's no fixing this one then?' he says.

Tomas's grin is friendly and suggests he knows there isn't. Two nights of heavy rain have fallen in through the open doors and windows, which has done nothing for the old estate, and it looks as though it has already started to sink into the verge behind the house. Tomas indicates the bag of tools he's brought up with him and waits for Timothy's go ahead. Timothy tries to conceal his surprise, but he nods and Tomas reaches in through the driver's door and pulls the catch for the bonnet beneath the steering wheel. He brings the bag of tools round to the front of the car and disappears beneath the bonnet, and Timothy stands at the kitchen door and fixes them both a coffee. As he drinks, Timothy becomes aware of how cold he had become sitting by the window for so long, despite the blanket he had pulled round his shoulders. There is some warmth in the sun that falls onto the back of the house and he stands on the step feeling the light rest on his face. Eventually, Tomas's voice rises up from within the silent engine.

'She's dead. Simple as that. She won't get you a mile let alone make the kind of journey you're looking to do.'

He comes out holding a piece of the engine in his hand and passes it to Timothy apologetically before returning to close the bonnet.

'Best you could do for her is point her in the direction of the sea and take the handbrake off, I reckon,' he says and smiles. 'I'd offer to take her off your hands, but she's a pile of junk.'

Timothy looks down at the blackened item in his hand. He is unable to identify it as something that plays an essential part in the running of an engine and he rolls it over back and forward in his hand, watching a streak of grease or dirt spread out across his palms and fingers. He hears Tomas is still talking to him and tunes back in.

'I could sort you something else out if it'll help?'

He nods at Tomas, who is packing his tools back into their bag and, as the fisherman starts to walk back into the village, he thanks him and Tomas raises a hand in response.

Later that afternoon, Timothy hears a car pull up outside Perran's, and then the reedy sound of its horn. Since Tomas had left him, Timothy had changed into the remaining clean clothes from the canvas bag and shaved in cold water from the kitchen sink, the only tap that seemed to be working. He feels slightly more human for it. Hearing the horn again, he walks through to the kitchen and sees Tomas waving at him through the windscreen of a car that makes the broken Volvo look practically new. The car Tomas has brought up to Perran's looks as though it has been welded together from thin sheets of metal that have been dragged up from the wreck of a ship. The bonnet and roof are almost totally clear of paint and the windows, too, look as though they have been scoured over and again with wire wool.

'She's a bit of a beach wreck, a bit sandblasted, but she's a runner,' Tomas says and he slaps the roof as if to prove his point. As he does so, the engine note dips a little and Timothy wonders for a moment whether it is going to give out completely, but it picks up again a few seconds later and Tomas's grin towards him broadens. Timothy looks in through the side window, shielding his eyes from the glare from the white sky reflected in it. The interior is all plastic leather effect. It is ripped and worn through in patches and cheap yellow foam sticks out from the gashes in the seats. Beneath the plastic steering wheel, wires of varying colours hang loosely and the handbrake sticks up from the floor, bare metal. He stands up and looks at Tomas across the roof. Tomas is still grinning.

'Looks as though someone's rolled it a few times,' says Timothy, running a hand over the uneven roof panels.

'That's possible,' replies Tomas. 'It's my sister's. She's got no use for it now. Never was the most careful driver. Could be why she lost her licence, come to think of it. Either way, she doesn't drive it any more and you'll not find much else here. Just sits down on the front most times, hence the slightly washed-out look. She's a runner though and yours if you want her.'

He waits for a response from Timothy and when it does not come, he continues.

'There's not a garage for miles and if there's another car going in the village, I'll be surprised.'

Timothy walks around the outside of the car and plays the buyer, though he knows there's little other choice. He flinches when Tomas gives him the price. Tomas shrugs his shoulders and gives him a look that tells him take it or leave it. Timothy pays with what cash he has left and after showing him how to start the engine by crossing two of the loose wires hanging beneath the dashboard, Tomas walks back down into the village, leaving the car ticking over on the road at the back of the house.

When Tomas has gone, Timothy gets into the driver's seat and feels the body of the car sink beneath him, though whether it is the springs beneath the seat or the car's suspension that cause this he cannot tell. He checks the switches for the lights and the few other controls on the plastic dashboard, though the lights do not seem to work at all and only one of the windscreen wipers functions, scraping slowly across the windscreen. He pushes a few buttons on the stereo and succeeds in getting only a loud static howl through one of the speakers. Standing on the doorframe, he looks around for an aerial and finds a rust-edged hole where one might have been. He gets back in and pulls his jumper sleeve up over his right hand and tries to clear the windscreen with it, but ends up smearing dirt around it, and when he reaches his hand round onto the outside of the windscreen, he can feel beneath his fingertips the scars left by the sand the wind carries with it from miles and miles away, from another country or another continent.

*'Timothy, he's gone.'*

*He had taken his wife's words in silence.*

*'Can you come, Timothy, please?'*

*There is nothing for a while then, save a few shards; seeing himself standing on his neighbour's doorstep knocking, hoping* they are in, and would they do him a favour and drive him over to the hospital; staring out of the windscreen as the red lights stretch out along the road in front of him and asking himself what he can do to make this right.

When he arrives at the hospital, there is a midwife waiting for him in the hallway and in the tiny room by which she stands he finds Lauren with a doctor explaining what will happen next, handing them both forms to sign, consent for procedures only some of which he has heard of.

The delivery room is dimmed and the midwife busies herself in the corner, filling in forms, moving papers from one pile to another. They have been there for hours now, maybe. Timothy is at his wife's head whispering he does not know what, smoothing her hair with one hand, his other clutched tight in hers. The midwife only raises her head when Lauren's breathing becomes laboured and, when she looks up at them, he wonders what it is she sees.

The room is quiet and in between contractions Lauren tries to sleep, though he sees the morphine is making her too sick to close her eyes for long. In one hand she has the controls for the drug and in the other she holds his hand and compresses each from time to time as if to check they are both still there. She talks to him, though what she says he does not remember and he knows his words back to her are just a voice that she recognises. He thinks they are telling each other stories, stories with different endings, stories that confirm and console.

'It's a boy.'

The midwife's accent is soft, Spanish or Latin American, and Timothy has the urge to tell her he has always wanted to visit Colombia or Bolivia. He smiles, though it is a smile he has not known before: a boy. The midwife offers him the scissors and stretches the cord a little for him to cut. He is a father again and he smiles and asks to hold his son.

Outside the window is a courtyard, though it is empty of patients, a small area for smokers with a bench beneath a bare tree.

When the midwife returns with Perran, they have dressed him in blue, with a hat pulled down over his head and secured with a blue ribbon tied beneath his chin, blue to match the dark blue of his lips. It is not what he would have chosen for his son, too fussy.

Later, while Lauren sleeps, he picks Perran out of the crib they have arranged for him and holds him to his chest. He tells him stories about his mother and then he sleeps a little in the chair in the corner of the room and when he wakes, he watches his wife and son through long hours.

There are more forms, a birth certificate, a death certificate, an apologetic doctor with a stack of papers that need to be read and processed, signed and dated, but mostly long periods of waiting. He sees the word autopsy and knows they are going to ask them to hand over their son though not yet – when you are ready. He signs and dates, signs and dates and then the doctor is gone for a while.

Lauren asks can their son stay with them overnight and the nurse looks pained and she says no, that is not possible, but they will bring him back up to the room in the morning.

Lauren lies back on the thin hospital bed and Timothy tries to make himself comfortable on the armchair in the corner of the room. The chair has a small brass plaque attached to it that says it was donated by a patient some years ago. It is a model that reclines, though the mechanism is broken and throughout the night the chair tries to return itself to its upright position and he gives up trying to sleep on it.

In the morning, they ask for their son back after a night of sleep and no sleep, a night listening to the muffled sounds from the ward outside and the tapping of a bare branch against the window. They wait for what seems an age and when the nurses bring Perran in Timothy takes him from the plastic crib and

*touches his son's forehead. It is ice cold, as are the tiny feet he
can feel against his arm. He holds his son to his chest for a while,
though whether this is to take away some of the cold or to pass
over his own warmth he does not know.*

*Later still, a midwife returns and tells them they can have
all the time they need, though when she leaves, she stays in the
corridor outside the room, which means there is less time. He feels
something stretch as he hands Perran over and it is all he can do
not to take him back. The best he can do is to ask them to treat
him with compassion. The midwife promises – they always do,
she says – and he watches her retreat along the corridor until she
turns off the ward with their son.*

Timothy taps the fuel gauge. The needle rests on a pin below
the empty line and does not respond to his tapping, and he
wonders how far the car will get him. He shuts off the engine
and returns to the house.

*The funeral director's parlour is little more than a shack in the
heart of a sprawling housing estate. Timothy and Lauren drive
past it twice and have to stop for directions, though no one seems
to have heard of it. They find it eventually, wedged between a
used car lot and a general store that has crates piled up outside
it, crates overflowing with vegetables, boxes of cleaning utensils,
cloths, tins, and children's watering cans in the shape of elephants.
The building itself is a prefabricated hut that looks as though it
may once have been a car dealership; they can see, beneath the
newer lettering, the evidence of its past life. The hut is raised up
on breezeblocks and enclosed within a small compound with a
high metal gate and fences topped with barbed wire. After they
have parked the car they walk up the metal steps into a small
waiting area, where a receptionist tells them Bob will be with
them soon. They sit on moulded plastic chairs that look as though*

*they have been requisitioned from a school and try not to listen in to the conversation they can hear going on behind the inner door. The receptionist smiles at them over the counter.*

*Five minutes later, the door opens and a couple walks out. Lauren and Timothy have to stand to allow them to manoeuvre around them to leave. Through the open door, the funeral director ushers them into his office. He is overweight, and sits behind a desk around which it looks as though he has trouble navigating. On their way through, the floor sways slightly beneath their feet and Timothy notices they have passed across a divide where two parts of the hut have been bolted together. While the funeral director talks to them, Timothy finds he cannot take his attention away from a stain on the man's white shirt, the remains of a lunch he ate at the desk perhaps. The strip lighting above them buzzes loudly and when they are ushered out, Timothy is aware of arrangements having been made, but he cannot bring any of the details to mind. He asks the girl sitting behind the desk in the cramped reception area if she will send him a copy of what they have agreed and she nods and smiles as though it's a common request. Outside, the remainder of the day's light has faded, and when they get beyond the boundary of the small compound, someone closes the heavy metal gate behind them. The yellow light flooding onto the pavement from the shop next door mingles with the music the shopkeeper in the general store has put on since they arrived.*

## 22

# *Ethan*

E THAN TRIES TO ignore the lines. At first, he rubs at his eyes and hopes, when the water clears from them, that the cracks will be gone. But they remain. The lines run in all directions where they emerge from the sea. At first it seems to Ethan as though they do not intersect – that they run parallel to each other, but gradually they grow in number and he sees the lines start to splinter soon after the point at which they leave the water and cross each other, over and again as if they are multiplying before him. The lines run up through the stones on the beach and into the village, hairline fractures that run and spread throughout the fabric of the whole place. He is not sure why, but he feels sure that, thin as they are, these cracks are signs of fissures too deep to contemplate. Down by the water's edge they now resemble a tangle of incredibly fine gill nets laid one on top of the other. Ethan retreats up off the beach and across into the village and for a while finds peace, though it is not long before he sees the first cracks appearing in the walls and ceiling of the pub.

He can feel the village starting to break up. He knows for sure, too, that the cracks run through the decks and the holds of the container ships on the horizon and that thought gives him some comfort. He tries to talk with the others about it, wants to point them out to Rab or Jory, but he finds, when he tries, the words will not form in his mouth and he must keep them to himself, since no one else talks of them either.

The lines proliferate. Dark and thin scars on the sand, the concrete, running through windows and doors. Over the course of the day they spread from the land onto the villagers themselves, across the bodies and faces of everyone around him. In a fit of panic, Ethan pulls at his sleeves and sees the white scars on his forearms have spread too, and now run the length of his arms and he knows without looking they now spread across his skin. He can feel them spread inside him too, through his muscles and bones and all his tissues until his body is alive with lines. They spread through what dreams he has when he manages to sleep and after a while they are all he sees, criss-cross scars running through the fabric of everything, running through all the seen and the unseen.

The only place that is free of the cracks is the sea itself, as though it is somehow immune to them, as if, even though they emanate from the sea, they are not of the sea. He takes to looking at the water for longer and longer periods, trying to calm himself, though the lines are now starting to cover the lenses of his eyes and no amount of blinking or rubbing at them makes a difference. Towards the end of the day he starts to hear a sound coming from within the fissures, though it is faint and whispered and if he stares at the sea hard enough, he is able to block out the noise for a while. And faint though it is, he recognises the sound, recognises it as a voice he knows almost as well as he knows his own. He strains to hear the words the voice is speaking but it is too distant for him to make anything out, too deep within the cracks.

He stays on the beach looking at the water until darkness falls hard enough to mask the lines on his skin and on the stones. As it gets later, he realises all there is to tell him they are still there is the faint sound that is so soft yet can be heard above the white noise of the waves.

He puts his ear to the ground and listens and after a while the sound of the waves ceases entirely and he is able to hear the voice from within the cracks clearly then. Soft and insistent as the moving of the air, though there are still no words that form, and he presses his ear to the cold ground hard. As he does so, Timothy's question comes back to him, 'Who was Perran?' And the feeling he cannot answer this question is one he is unable to describe, but now he has thought it, it seems to come, too, from the cracks in the surface of everything.

# 23

# Timothy

THEIR SON ARRIVES *in a small black people carrier, accompanied by a man and a woman, who, in any other setting, would look like bankers or lawyers. Timothy approaches the car as it pulls up beneath the overhanging roof by the chapel door. The pair get out of the car and open the car boot and when he sees them waiting there and looking over at him, Timothy comes round to join them at the back of the car. He is surprised when the man asks if he wants to carry the coffin into the chapel. It is not something he had considered before this moment and the men have already made a space for him at the car's open boot. He nods, and a few minutes later, when both his and Lauren's families have gathered, he takes the small coffin from the waiting man and carries it in his arms to where a chaplain he has not seen before is standing by the open door to the chapel.*

*When they emerge from the service, Timothy looks around him and blinks in the hard light. To one side the chimney and red-brick sharpness of the crematorium walls, to the other silver and bronze plaques which run the length of a low wall on which another family are already sitting, waiting their turn. Beyond the wall the uniformity of the memorial garden stretches out. Small white markers, regimented and even, lead his eyes to a dark line of trees, which mark the boundary of the cemetery. The chaplain leads them through the garden to a small clearing, at the*

*centre of which is a larger white memorial. Laid around it are*
*toy bears, plastic toys, cards, flowers, all wrapped in cellophane*
*against the rain. As they head towards it, Timothy holds back*
*from the rest of the gathering and the chaplain slows his pace a*
*little.*

*'Will there be any ashes for us to scatter?' he asks.*

*'No. I'm afraid that won't be possible,' the chaplain replies.*
*'Not with a child that small. It's not possible.'*

*The chaplain continues talking to him and Timothy tries to*
*concentrate on what he is saying but cannot block out the low*
*roar of the motorway beyond the trees and cannot fix the words*
*being spoken to him and they drift away.*

*Later, back at home, he tries to bring to mind his son, but all*
*his memory can return for him is the sight of the crematorium*
*tower, the dull roar of the motorway like surf on the sand, and*
*the sense of being hemmed in on all sides.*

Timothy walks through the house and removes the dustsheets
from the furniture and the carpets. It does not surprise him
somehow that the damage he should expect to see, that was so
viscerally present only hours earlier, has gone, that the house
has reclaimed itself even from this attack. He walks up the
stairs and again it is no surprise to him that the plasterwork
on the walls all the way up the stairs has reverted to how it
was when he first arrived. The same watermarks show through
on the walls and ceilings. He has the sensation that when he
walks away from the house for the final time, any memory he
currently holds of it will fade completely and he will be unable
to describe it to Lauren at all, what it was like to be here, to
live in this place for so long. He wonders whether the same will
be true of his memories of the village as a whole, that all that
has taken place since he arrived would fade. As he looks out of
the window in the small bedroom towards the sea, he runs his

fingers along the windowpane and flecks of dried paint peel off beneath his fingertips.

*It's hard to get rid of fresh cut flowers. They come in waves after the first couple of days, as news gets round. They arrive in bunches of bunches, and each delivery driver who knocks greets them with a smile and congratulates them as they open the door to receive yet more. More cut flowers than he has ever seen in one place outside a florist's. After the spare shelves and windowsills are taken, the kitchen units fill, the sink, and eventually two buckets on the kitchen floor. They are crowded in by the flowers and thoughts of people they know well and those they barely know, by relatives neither of them has spoken to in years and by neighbours who bring plates of food and yet more flowers.*

*When the flowers get too much, Timothy looks up the addresses of all the local care homes and notes them down on the back of an envelope. He waits until the majority of their neighbours have left for work, and fills the car with the flowers, still in their cellophane collars and coloured paper wrappings. He has tried to make sure he has removed all the little cards that accompany each of the bouquets, and he checks each of them in turn as he lays them in the boot and, when the boot is full, the back seats and the front passenger seat of the car. He follows a route that takes him in a circle around the edge of the town, stopping at each of the addresses he has listed on the envelope in turn. A man stops him as he is walking up the driveway of one of the smaller care homes with several bunches in his hands, and Timothy is surprised when he asks how much he wants for the flowers. When Timothy replies he is giving them away, the man looks at him with suspicion and says he will only take one bunch, as though he imagines an invoice will be pushed through the door later. As he returns home, there are still several bouquets in the boot of the car and he drops them off outside a small and deserted Catholic church at the turning*

*into his road. The church is a modern one and the entrance is all*
*plate glass with light wood for the window frames and the desk*
*in the entrance hall. In the hall stands a faded plaster Virgin*
*Mary, who looks out of place standing alone on the expanse of*
*office carpet in the vestibule, looking as though she belongs in*
*another place altogether. She stares out into the empty car park*
*with sad eyes. He leaves the remaining bunches of flowers outside*
*the locked door, though he is sure, when they are discovered, they*
*will be swept up into a bin, but he is too tired of the flowers to*
*return with them.*

The village is quiet, and the sun is just starting to set, the full-
ness of its orb just beginning to flatten at the bottom against
the horizon. Timothy can make out, over the rooftops and
twisting streets that run down to the water below, dark specks
on the water that are the boats of the fleet, spread out across the
sea. He looks out beyond the boats to where the sun's light is
brightest on the water, and it takes a while for him to realise the
container ships punctuating the horizon seem more distant now,
further away than they had been before. He wonders whether
perhaps they will continue to drift out and eventually they
will drop off the edge altogether. Or whether perhaps they will
return later in greater numbers.

He looks around at the front room and it occurs to him
again that the house is as unfamiliar to him now as it was
when he arrived, as strange and unforgiving as it has been to
him all along. And he is certain, when he leaves, this space will
change again. It will change again beyond his recognition, and
if he was to return to the house at some point in his future, he
knows it would not be the same place in which he stands now.
The coals in the grate are glowing their last and he uses an iron
poker to move them around and help them on their way, and
he feels beneath his thin socks the frayed carpet where the fire

must have spat out hot embers. He does and does not want to leave this place. But Lauren is not coming. He has been talking to her at a distance for weeks, but it is only now he registers what she has been saying to him. That she is waiting for him at the home they share.

As the last of the embers fade to black, he has a brief waking dream that the sea has pulled itself in again, up the hill towards Perran's house. Or that Perran's house is somehow pulling itself forward towards the sea, compressing the space between the two, willing itself towards the water. That this place is the site of a battle long fought between the sea and the land and the inhabitants of this place. The sensation is so strong that he gets up and goes to the window and stares out into the bright cold daylight to see if he can perceive any difference in either the village or the sea, but everything looks calm now, as it was when he first arrived. And though the white flecks on the waves in the distance may be a fury of confusion closer up, from up here, and now, the sea looks benign.

He tries to put the thought to one side, and when it will not shift he walks upstairs and retrieves the canvas bag from the bed. He leaves the house by the kitchen door and this time closes it behind him before going to the car.

He throws the bag in through the car door onto the passenger seat and stands leaning against the thin doorframe. His old estate has already started to become part of the landscape, and for a moment he has the strong sensation that the rotting car is the only sign he will leave that he has been in this place.

He gets in and connects the leads beneath the dashboard to start the engine. It coughs into life. He taps the control panel again, but there is no response. The fuel gauge still reads empty. He tests the one working wiper to clear some of the rain from the windscreen, but that too is now not working.

Timothy drives slowly down through the village, and as he

passes by, he sees few of the villagers in the streets, and the ones he sees have a look of panic, as though they fear some inevitable change that is about to occur. As he passes the tightly packed cottages, he can see in through open doors, people shifting furniture. Whether they are preparing for another high tide or for something else he does not know, and cannot ask. Though he can see nothing in the village that has changed, the small streets feel narrower, the houses less substantial somehow, and the journey between Perran's and the beach road feels compressed, shortened. As he drives, almost at walking pace, he looks behind himself several times, though there is no one following him and no one paying attention to his movements.

As he gets closer to the beach, he sees several people he recognises from the mob the week before, but they are all too concerned with their own business to register him. The stares on those he passes are blank and without recognition. The sense of watchfulness he has had over the past few weeks and months has faded, as though everyone is going about their jobs now, as though he is no longer their concern.

He does not stop at the beach and does not look to see whether Clem has resumed his post on the step of the winch house, but instead fixes his gaze onto the road that lifts up from that point, along the coast and away from the village.

It is as the road starts to rise that the engine starts to struggle. There is no power in it and he knows, even before the road becomes steeper, the car is never going to make it to the top of the rise. It is over quickly. The engine does not put up much of a fight, just coughs a couple of times and then it cuts out completely. After a moment the car starts to roll back down towards the village and he pulls on the handbrake, which slows it down, and then he jams the wheel over to one side, so the car comes to a rest against the verge.

He gets out and takes the canvas bag from the passenger

seat before carefully closing the car doors, and he walks up the steep hill away from the village. At the top he sees the woman in grey again, standing some way off beside her car, and it occurs to him that maybe she is standing guard over them. He wonders whether she has left her post out on the coast road since the waters rose. Even from a distance, he sees, despite the intensity of her gaze, that she looks tired and worn. She must stay somewhere to sleep or at least to rest, he thinks, though he cannot picture her staying in the village. Usually she is either standing or leaning against the bonnet, staring in towards the village centre, or out towards the boats as they leave the cove and when they return to the shore.

Timothy walks on towards her, out of the lee of the hill and he feels the wind howl in from the sea. It is strong and he lowers his gaze and puts a hand up in front of his face, and walks on towards her. As he gets closer he realises he has lost sight of the woman and he assumes she has got into the car and is now sitting behind the tinted glass windows. When he walks round in front of the car, though, he sees she is not there and he walks further, around the bonnet, and finds her kneeling down on the tarmac beside the car. She is praying perhaps, or crying. As he gets closer still he sees she is doing neither, but instead is tracing patterns on the surface of the road with the tip of her forefinger, lines which run in several directions, which intersect and run across each other. She does not turn towards him then or raise her head as he approaches, though he feels she is aware of him approaching.

When he is within a few feet of her he stops and observes her at her task, and when she does not acknowledge him, he turns around and looks out to sea while he waits for her to finish whatever it is she is doing.

## 24

# *Timothy*

THE FINE RAIN driving in from the sea has passed now, as though it was never there, but it has soaked through his thin jacket and Timothy looks to either side of him. To one side the village and to the other the road cutting a line between the empty sea and the empty fields. He stands between the two for some time before he realises the woman in grey has joined him and now she stands next to him, looking out from the verge beside the parked car.

The hood of her long coat is pulled up over her hair against the wind, but she is turned slightly towards him and Timothy can see her face clearly. While she must see him, she does not acknowledge him. She is watching something intently and he follows her gaze.

At first he thinks she is looking towards the horizon, where he sees the container ships have broken free of the great weight that had held them where they were, and they are now barely visible on the horizon and spread much further than they had been, almost invisible now in the distance.

But he feels his gaze being drawn back towards the shore and he sees that what she is watching is a boat in the middle distance, small in the mounting sea. Though the *Great Hope* is a way out, pitching on the unsettled water, Timothy sees the boat as if it is in close-up. He can feel it shift beneath his feet and beneath his fingers he feels the peeling paint and the crack in the window at the side of the wheelhouse and the nets laid out neatly on the crates, and he knows, though is unsure how this could be, that she is showing this to him somehow, that she is guiding his vision.

He sees Ethan standing out on the foredeck and feels the wind as it races across the waves and through Ethan's clothes and hair. As if he is aware he is being observed, or in answer to some silent cue, Ethan unbuttons his coat and lets it drop to the drenched deck, feeling the roll and the turn of the waves beneath the boat. Timothy watches Ethan as he lets the rest of his clothes fall and he stands still, making up his mind about something and it occurs to Timothy for a moment how similar he is to the other man. Ethan stands there still for a while longer and then climbs up over the crates that are piled in front of the wheelhouse, and up higher onto its small roof and he sways with the waves and the wind. He stands on the roof of the cabin and looks back towards the village. Timothy now realises he is seeing events not just through his own eyes but through Ethan's, too, and as he does, the fragile boundaries that held together for a short while begin to vibrate and blur.

Ethan then dives down from the roof of the boat into the water and Timothy can feel in his dive a grace, an economy of action that harmonises with something deep within him, and he experiences the dive as though he is both within Ethan's body and watching him from without.

The wind tugging at his clothes brings him back to the verge and he turns briefly towards the woman, who is looking out at the sea with an expression that he cannot read, but that is familiar to him. For a moment then she turns her head towards Timothy and meets his gaze. Her eyes impart something to him then, something that suggests she understands, and feeling wells up in him, so much so he feels he might be overwhelmed by it. The exchange between them is entirely silent.

Timothy returns his gaze to the sea for some time, looking for a sign of Ethan resurfacing, but there is nothing there now other than the abandoned boat amid the white peaks of the waves that spread out in all directions. When his eyes start to hurt from searching the waves, he shifts his focus once more to the *Great Hope*, and he watches it for a while as it bobs on the surface of the sea, aimless and without direction, before he turns away.

# Acknowledgments

H UGE THANKS TO Nick Royle for guidance, expertise and kindness and for genius book recommendations; to Nikita Lalwani and Sam North for early support and encouragement; to the fine writers on MMU's MA Creative Writing for their insightful comments and feedback, and in particular to Zoë Feeney and Joanne Phillips; to the fishermen who put up with my questions about nets and catches and who shared with me their stories of the sea; to Kate and Jonathan for my retreat on the creek and the teams at Totleigh Barton and Lumb Bank for giving me the time and space to write; to John Oakey for the excellent cover and Dave Muir for the photos; to Chris and Jen at Salt for being publishers extraordinaire; to Bec and Chris for a singularly useful piece of writing advice (it's 'finish what you start', in case you're interested); and to Em, Lana and Tom, for everything.

# NEW FICTION FROM SALT